DOUBLE JEOPARDY
STRENGHTH IN NUMBERS 1

By Rachel Bo

DOUBLE JEOPARDY
An Ellora's Cave Publication, January 2005

Ellora's Cave Publishing, Inc.
1337 Commerce Drive
Stow, Ohio 44224

ISBN #1-84360-951-7

Double Jeopardy © 2004 Rachel Bo
ISBN MS Reader (LIT) ISBN # 1-84360-854-5
Other available formats (no ISBNs are assigned):
Adobe (PDF), Rocketbook (RB), Mobipocket (PRC) & HTML

Edited by *Raelene Gorlinsky.*
Cover art by *Syneca*

What the critics are saying:

5 STARS! "...after reading this story, I will be on the look out for more from (Rachel Bo). Kendall is awesome...Josh and Sutter are two very sexy men...The sex in this book is to die for...I am really impressed by this author...definitely look forward to the next in this series." - *Julie Bryan, Just Erotic Romance Reviews*

"Double Jeopardy is beyond HOT!!...touching tale of love...well done and highly arousing...a fabulous book!" -*Amber Taylor, Just Erotic Romance Reviews*

"...delicious sexual encounters...wonderful job...handling both the older woman/younger men romance and the introduction of male/male sex into the relationship" - *Meribeth McCombs, The Road to Romance*

"...unique and powerful tale...one hell of a story...the characters are truly unforgettable, as is the name Rachel Bo."

- Tracey West, The Road to Romance

Warning:

The following material contains graphic sexual content meant for mature readers. *Double Jeopardy* has been rated *E-rotic* by a minimum of three independent reviewers.

Ellora's Cave Publishing offers three levels of Romantica™ reading entertainment: S (S-ensuous), E (E-rotic), and X (X-treme).

S-*ensuous* love scenes are explicit and leave nothing to the imagination.

E-*rotic* love scenes are explicit, leave nothing to the imagination, and are high in volume per the overall word count. In addition, some E-rated titles might contain fantasy material that some readers find objectionable, such as bondage, submission, same sex encounters, forced seductions, etc. E-rated titles are the most graphic titles we carry; it is common, for instance, for an author to use words such as "fucking", "cock", "pussy", etc., within their work of literature.

X-*treme* titles differ from E-rated titles only in plot premise and storyline execution. Unlike E-rated titles, stories designated with the letter X tend to contain controversial subject matter not for the faint of heart.

Also by Rachel Bo:

Ringing In The Season: 12 Quickies of Christmas
Symphony in Rapture

DOUBLE JEOPARDY
STRENGHTH IN NUMBERS 1

By Rachel Bo

Chapter One
Temptation

The first time they came into her shop, Kendall was struck by the contrast between them. One man stood tall and bronzed with short, straight hair painted a dozen different shades of blonde by the sun. He was muscular in a lean, athletic way and exuded a bright, casual confidence that literally seemed to light up the room. Eyes the darkest brown Kendall had ever seen were surrounded by indecently long lashes, and when Kendall met that gaze it was like drowning in molasses. She was sucked in so fast it took her breath away. A massive effort of will was required for her to smile politely and drag her attention from him to his companion.

Short. Olive-complected. Thick hair that was dark as midnight, shaggy curls just brushing his broad shoulders. His tank top revealed the large, well-defined muscles of a man who was into weight-lifting. Unlike his friend, there was an air of quiet reserve about him. Of shy withdrawal. She met his gaze and it was like diving into a whirlpool. His dark grey eyes were stormy waters and Kendall once again found herself struggling to look away, but there was an abiding calm beneath that dangerous surface. Kendall had a sudden sense that this man had weathered his storms and come through with an unshakable inner strength. It came to her that if the tall blonde were the foundation of a house, here was the bedrock upon which that foundation stood. She experienced an unexpected longing to be a part of that. She stared into his eyes, unable to look away until one of them cleared his throat.

What's wrong with me? Kendall thought. Never before had she reacted so strongly to a man. Hastily pulling herself together, she glanced from one to the other and asked, "May I help you?"

"*Lady of the Myths*," the taller one mused, referring to the name of her shop. "I like that."

Kendall smiled. "Thank you."

"How long have you been here?" he asked.

"The shop?"

He nodded.

"Oh, let's see. I moved here when I was twenty-three. Opened about a year later, so approximately eight years, I guess."

The tall man glanced at his companion. "I can't believe we never noticed it before." Then they were both staring at her again, an intense scrutiny so sultry that for a moment she imagined her clothes going up in flames, revealing her eager nipples, her damp crotch—shocked at herself, Kendall turned away.

Straightening a figurine that didn't need straightening, she stammered, "I-I'm not that surprised. Most of my customers are tourists, or couples looking to decorate a home." She took a deep, calming breath and turned back, determined to ignore the effect they were having on her. "I don't think you're tourists—you look more like locals. College students?" She raised her eyebrows questioningly. "Furnishing a dorm?"

"A home." The blonde met her gaze boldly. It seemed to Kendall as though he were trying to tell her something without coming right out and saying it. "Actually, it's just a house right now. With any luck it will be a home soon." For a fleeting moment, she thought he was trying to tell her that they were gay. That they were setting up house together and then it would be a home. But Kendall knew desire when she saw it, and they were both devouring her with their eyes. Their regard seemed to penetrate right down to her bones. Kendall shivered with a sudden urge to brush her tingling nipples against their chests. The dark man shared a glance with his tall companion, then stepped forward, close enough that if Kendall were to draw a deep breath, her fantasy would become a reality. It was almost as if he had read her mind. Startled, Kendall stepped back. He watched her with a secretive smile on his face.

Flustered, she looked up with relief as the bell on the shop door jangled and a couple entered. "Why don't you two look around, and call me if you need any help."

She went to greet the elderly man and woman and occupied herself with finding just the right mermaid accents for their newly remodeled bathroom. By the time she sent the couple on their way, the two men were gone.

Or so she thought. Later, when she had locked up and was reaching to pull the steel mesh gate down over the storefront, two sets of hands suddenly appeared to either side of hers. The tall blonde easily reached the handle Kendall was having difficulty grasping and he and his companion pulled the gate down and set the clamps.

"Thanks," Kendall said a trifle breathlessly.

Their eyes glittered, reflecting the glow of the streetlamps. "No problem."

Kendall turned to go, but the blonde reached out and touched her shoulder. "Let us take you to dinner."

Strange things were happening to Kendall's arm. Tiny electric shocks danced from his fingertips like lightning. She glanced down, almost expecting to see sparks, but of course there was nothing. Just his hand. Kendall felt a sudden vertigo. For a brief moment, it was as though she were looking at herself through this stranger's eyes. He wanted to pull the clip from her hair, run his fingers through her long tresses, caress her. Abruptly, she jerked her shoulder from his grasp. "No, thank you." She backed away, eyes wide, then turned and hurried to her car. Her hand shook as she let herself in, then slammed and locked the door, backing quickly out of the lot. When she glanced in her rear-view mirror, they were both still standing there, watching her drive away.

* * * * *

Kendall leaned back in the booth and studied her companion. Brandy worked part-time for Kendall in the shop and despite their almost ten-year age difference they'd become close friends. She was a senior at the University of Houston. Kendall had been surprised to find out she drove into Houston every day to attend college, but of the three universities in Galveston, only two offered four-year programs and both were very specialized — the University of Texas at Galveston offering medical degrees, and the branch of Texas A&M offering only marine-related degrees. Brandy and many of her friends made the one-hour drive every day in order to obtain the degree of their choice. Kendall sipped at her strawberry shake as she watched Brandy polish off the last of their chili-cheese fries. *Actually*, she mused to herself, *we're about as unlikely a pair as those two guys in the shop earlier.*

It was true. Brandy was young, outgoing, petite — the kind of girl who could eat an elephant and never gain a pound. Her pale blond hair was blunt-cut just below her ears, that and her dimples giving her a pixie-like quality that Kendall found endearing. It had also been extremely useful. Kendall had utilized Brandy several times now as a model for her fantasy paintings and next month one of their collaborations would be on the cover of a new fantasy novel.

Kendall felt like an elephant sometimes, next to Brandy. She was of average height but felt overly tall in comparison to her diminutive friend. And she would never be mistaken for slender. Kendall had always been active — hiking, biking, swimming. But despite her active lifestyle, she'd always been heavy. People seemed to think that if a person was overweight, they were lazy. Consequently, Kendall found herself continually surprising acquaintances with her strength and stamina. She had tried dieting when she was younger, but gave it up when it became obvious to her that her size actually had little to do with how much she did or did not eat. In her opinion, plump and happy was infinitely better than thin and irritable. Being overweight certainly hadn't stopped her from becoming a success. She had moved to the coast — fulfilling a life-long dream — and opened her own shop, which was doing quite well. And now with her artwork in demand both privately and commercially, her career as an artist was finally gaining momentum and she was as happy as she'd ever been.

Well, almost. She still missed her brother terribly. Her brother was the only person in her past that had not let her down, and she had to admit to herself that she still harbored that dream of finding someone like him. A good man, solid and reliable, with whom she could build a quiet, comfortable life.

For some reason, that thought brought to mind again her young male visitors. Just picturing them set her pulse racing. It came to her that if they were college students, Brandy might know them. She stirred her shake with her straw, mentioning idly, "I had an interesting encounter in the shop today."

Brandy swallowed the last of her soda and looked up. "Really?"

"Yeah." Kendall related the odd experience, describing the two men, but left out the incident that had occurred as she was locking up.

Brandy pursed her lips. "Hmmm. That sounds like Sutter Campbell and Joshua Reed." Brandy had grown up in Galveston and seemed to Kendall to have at least a passing acquaintance with everyone living within a hundred miles of the place. Not really surprising, given her looks, generous nature and outgoing personality.

"Know anything about them?" Kendall asked casually.

Brandy grinned and raised an eyebrow. "Why do you ask?"

Kendall felt heat rising in her cheeks. "Just curious."

Brandy smiled a knowing smile. "Sure. They both go to the University of Houston. Sutter's very popular. He's pre-law. The one person everyone invites to their parties. There's not a guy on campus who doesn't like him—hell, they want to *be* him. And the girls..." She ticked off his features on her fingers. "He's funny, his dad's very well-off, *and* he's gorgeous. They're all trying to get their hooks into him.

"Now, Josh I don't know that much about. He's studying architecture, I think. He and Sutter are best friends—practically inseparable." She paused for a moment, wiping chili from her lips. "He's quiet. Sutter does most of the talking. People include Josh because he's, like, permanently attached to Sutter. As a matter of fact, the rumor when they were freshmen was that they were gay."

Kendall thought about the way they'd been looking at her that afternoon and frowned as a sultry heat flooded her groin. *This is insane,* she thought. *You're thirty-two years old and these are college kids. They can't possibly be interested in you.* But she couldn't seem to help herself. She had to know. "What do you think?"

Brandy shook her head. "No way! I've seen the way they look at women. Besides, Sutter has dated some of my friends and they tell me he's *definitely* not gay."

"Really? What do they say?"

Brandy grinned wolfishly. "They say that even if he weren't handsome and loaded they'd go out with him again just for the hot sex. But that's the thing. He never asks. He hasn't dated a girl twice yet, and he's graduating this year!"

"Have you gone out with him?"

Brandy made a face. "Nah. There's something odd about him. It's like he's looking for something. He's got this air of expectancy, and it didn't disappear when we met. I knew right away I wasn't for him and he wasn't for me. It was kind of strange, actually. I've never been so certain about a guy before."

Kendall slurped up the dregs of her shake, mulling that over in her head. Setting the cup aside, she asked, "What about Joshua?"

Brandy said, "He doesn't date much. I know a couple of girls — they said he was incredibly shy. Hardly spoke two words all evening and didn't even kiss them good night." She chuckled. "You know what, though? They both wanted to go out with him again. Tammy said — hmmm, how did she put it? That there were 'hidden currents' in him. I guess some gals just go for that quiet, mysterious type."

Kendall nodded thoughtfully.

"So why the third degree?" Brandy prompted. "You got a crush on one of them?"

Again, Kendall felt her cheeks growing hot. "Of course not." She averted her eyes, staring out the café window at the breakers rolling in across the gulf. The truth of the matter was, she wasn't sure *what* was going on with her. She had never in her life felt the way she had that afternoon. *Josh and Sutter,* she mused. She knew instinctively that they wanted something from her. Exactly what, she was reluctant to consider.

Kendall sighed and turned back to find Brandy observing her shrewdly. "What?!" Kendall asked tartly.

The petite blonde raised both eyebrows and held up her hands as though fending off a blow. "Nothing, nothing. If you don't want to tell me what's going on, that's fine."

Kendall rolled her eyes. "There's nothing to tell."

Brandy grinned as she picked up her purse and burrowed in search of change to pay her half of the tab. "Sure, Kendall. Whatever you say."

Chapter Two
Arousal

Kendall tried hard to concentrate on the sketch she was working on, but she could feel their eyes devouring her and she couldn't focus. Wherever she went, Sutter and Josh seemed to appear like magic. Watching her with those mesmerizing eyes in restaurants. Following her as she walked along the boardwalk. Brushing up against her at parties and in crowded bars, their touch engendering an aching erotic need, the contact again seeming to communicate thoughts and desires that came from outside herself. They even haunted her dreams. Kendall blushed furiously as she remembered some of the things they had done in those dreams. For three months she'd been in a near-constant state of arousal. She couldn't take it any more.

Get it over with, the voice in her head prompted. Kendall rubbed her temples. *You have to be crazy to even consider this*, she argued with herself. *They're just BOYS, for Christ's sake!* But she had to do *something*. A strange awareness had been growing within her daily. A conviction that had her by turns both excited and apprehensive. The feeling that for whatever reason, Sutter and Josh both wanted her and that they meant for it to be a package deal.

She had sounded Brandy out, fishing for hints that they had done anything like this before, but apparently they had not. There were no ménage à trois rumors floating around about the two of them. And yet, Kendall was convinced that was what they wanted. And heaven help her, she wanted it too.

It's now or never, Kendall, that voice in her head goaded. *Are you a woman or a wimp?* Swallowing past the nervous lump in her throat, Kendall closed her sketchbook. Gathering up her supplies, she stuck them in her bag and stood, brushing the sand from her lap. Bending over, she picked up her beach towel and folded it carefully, aware every moment of their eyes on her. Watching. Waiting. Taking a deep breath, Kendall turned and marched purposefully up the sandy incline toward the bench where they were seated.

Sutter nudged Josh with his elbow. Kendall faltered as they both stared at her. Then Sutter smiled. It was an open, welcoming grin that inspired instant response, and Kendall found herself smiling back. He stood and waved her onto the bench, settling himself cross-legged on the ground before it.

"Kendall." Sutter's entire body tingled, just having her so near after waiting so long. He drank in the sight of her. A heart-shaped face that lit up when she smiled. Wavy chocolate-brown locks entwined with auburn strands and caught at the nape of her neck in a large silver clip which only slightly tamed the thick fall. A voluptuous, rubenesque figure whose curves offered the sweet promise of hours of exploratory pleasure.

Kendall licked her lips nervously. Sutter shifted as intense need flooded the area between his legs at this tantalizing glimpse of her soft, wet tongue. He shared a significant look with Josh. "We've never formally met," she said, holding out her hand. "Kendall Aaronson."

Sutter didn't shake her hand. He reached out with both of his and caressed it. Kendall's heart did a somersault and pounded against her ribcage like a monkey trying to escape the zoo. "It's great to finally meet you," he murmured. Startled at the strength of her reaction, Kendall pulled away from his grasp and turned slightly, offering her outstretched hand to Josh. He took it in his and brought it up to his lips, planting a soft kiss on her knuckle. Kendall suppressed a wild impulse to pull him close, to feel those lips against hers. Joshua smiled suddenly. Leaning forward, he kissed her gently.

Josh had to fight to keep from closing his eyes and drowning in the rush of erotic heat the touch of Kendall's flesh excited in him. *She's almost ours*, he thought. *But she's scared*. He felt her tense, and sensed she was on the verge of changing her mind and running away. He sat back. Staring deep into her eyes, he shook his head slightly. For several moments they remained that way, with Kendall poised on the edge of flight. Joshua watched the play of emotions in the depths of her green-flecked, golden-brown eyes. With her hand still clasped in his, Josh felt everything she was feeling. How much she was drawn to them both — but also how uncomfortable she was with this strong attraction to two different men, and with the idea of giving herself to both of them. And yet, underneath it all — Joshua let his mind slip into the red pool of Kendall's desire.

Kendall gasped. Something like a bolt of lightning danced within her, a storm making its way back and forth between the two of them through their linked hands. Sensations and longings that she knew did not belong to her. Kendall tried to break the contact, but Joshua held her hand tight. "Don't run away," he whispered. "We've been looking for you for such a long time." She was vaguely aware of Sutter taking her other hand and the riot increased, two strangers' thoughts and emotions racing through her veins. An overwhelming, almost painful tightness invaded her crotch. Kendall shifted restlessly. *No, wait — oh, my God!* That was Sutter and Josh. Kendall whimpered as she felt through them the sweet torment of an engorged cock and her pussy wept in response, warmth trickling between her legs.

Before he could stop himself, Josh closed his eyes, the better to savor Kendall's delicious response. With eye contact broken, the tumult began to fade into the background and Kendall again became aware of her sweaty palm clasped in Joshua's hand. Regaining a sense of self, she was able to withdraw from the stream of consciousness flowing between them. "What was that?" she mumbled. The men exchanged glances. Joshua ran his thumb across the back of her hand, sending a tremor through her body. "Maybe we could discuss it over dinner?"

Kendall's blood sang with the memory of desire — hers, his, Sutter's. She couldn't believe what she was about to say, yet she said it anyway. She took a deep breath. "I have a better idea," she murmured huskily. "Let's go to my place."

Sutter jumped up eagerly, but Josh hesitated, studying her. "Are you sure about this?"

Kendall shook her head. "Not really." Then she met his eyes and said, "But let's go anyway." Josh nodded, and they walked over and climbed into Sutter's convertible.

"So, where am I headed?"

"Back to the shop."

A few minutes later, Sutter pulled into the parking lot. Kendall got out and led them toward the back of the building. "I live in an apartment above the gallery," she explained as she started up a set of stairs that ended in a balcony. At the landing, she unlocked the door, stepped in and turned on the light. "Come on in."

Kendall locked the door behind them. "Have a seat," she offered. Sutter sat in a recliner near the fireplace, and Joshua sat on the couch. Suddenly at a loss, she cast about for something to say. "How does coffee sound?"

"Sounds good," Josh replied. He got up quickly from the couch. "Can I help?"

"Thanks."

Kendall went into the kitchen and turned on the coffee pot, achingly aware of Josh's potent masculinity in the tiny space. He investigated the cabinets until he found the cups. "How do you like your coffee?" he asked.

"Two teaspoons of sugar, and a dash of milk."

Josh grinned. "Me too," he said. "Sutter takes three teaspoons." He measured sugar into their cups, then stirred as Kendall poured in the coffee. Kendall grabbed the milk from the refrigerator and added a little to each cup, then she and Josh joined Sutter in the living room.

The sun was setting and the evening had become chilly.

Sutter pointed at the fireplace. "Do you mind?" Kendall shook her head, and moments later Sutter had a small blaze dancing on the grate. Kendall sat on the sofa and Josh took a seat right beside her. She could feel the heat of him even through their jeans. *What am I doing?* she thought.

Josh sensed her anxiety and sipped his coffee nonchalantly, trying to put her at ease. "This is good."

"Thanks." Kendall tried to ignore the spreading wetness in her crotch — sipping at her coffee, staring into the fire to avoid their intense scrutiny. As time stretched on, so did her nerves, until she thought her limbs might snap if she tried to move.

To her relief, Sutter finally broke the silence.

"Josh and I met in third grade." He looked up and grinned. "We were best friends right away. Practically lived at each other's houses." At a glance from Josh, he clarified. "Well, I spent a lot of time at *his* house, anyway.

"It was a while before we realized we could — *feel* each other the way you just experienced." He captured her gaze with his. "We've never been able to do that with a single other person, until you."

Kendall's heart raced. Already, she was longing to regain that touch — that frighteningly intimate contact. To cover her confusion, she leaned forward and set her empty cup on the table.

"The first time we saw you, we knew." He glanced at Josh again. Setting his own cup aside, he got up and came to kneel in front of her. "We're soul mates, Kendall. The three of us. Josh and I have always known there was something — some*one* — missing, and here you are. You're a part of us."

Kendall thought for a moment. Her heart was saying *yes*, recalling the instant connection she had felt to both these men, but her mind was saying *this is crazy*. "How can you be so sure?"

Josh cleared his throat and then both he and Sutter were holding out their hands. The thought of baring her soul to them again was frightening; and yet inexorably, like iron drawn to a magnet, Kendall reached out to clasp their strong hands with cold, tentative fingers.

A flash of triumph danced along her nerves. *Sutter*, Kendall thought. Unorganized, passionate, impulsive, his thoughts flickered into being and then disappeared almost as rapidly. Bold and confident, even a trifle arrogant. And yet — *wanting* her, even *needing* her, steeling himself against the possibility of rejection.

Josh, on the other hand, was just as she had imagined in the store — his thoughts confident, solid, unshakeable. And all of that buoyed by an undercurrent of total conviction and a joy that pierced her to the very core — a sense of finally being whole.

And in that instant, some part of Sutter and Josh slipped into place inside her, like the missing pieces of a puzzle. Her body shook with the force of it — an utter sense of belonging.

Overwhelmed, Kendall pulled her hands from their grasp. She leaned back into the cushions, trembling. Sutter stood and moved to stand behind the couch. Kendall jumped a little as his lean fingers began to massage her shoulders. At first she tensed, but the bond was quiet and his touch was so welcome, so relaxing, she finally went limp. "Mmmm, that feels good." She rested her head against the cushions and closed her eyes.

The couch shuddered slightly as Josh moved. His fingers began to knead her thighs, just above the kneecaps. Kendall opened her eyes and started to sit up, but Sutter pushed her back into the couch. "Shhhh," he whispered in her ear. "We won't do anything you don't want us to do. Just enjoy." Kendall sighed and closed her eyes again.

Josh's fingers on the tops of her thighs were slow tendrils of flame, working their way up toward her hips. Sutter's hands massaged her shoulders gently, melting her resistance, slipping slowly, seductively, lower and lower; until Kendall's nipples stiffened in response, her top's rough weave scratching the upright peaks through her thin lace bra as he massaged the upper swell of each breast. Kendall moaned softly. A mantle of heat enveloped her shoulders, her breasts, her rib cage. Josh pushed her legs apart slightly, massaging the inner portion of her thighs, the tips of his fingers tantalizingly close to her tingling crotch.

Sutter smiled to himself as Kendall's back arched and her breath quickened. He glanced at Josh. Sutter didn't want to scare Kendall off at this point by being too aggressive. But Josh nodded, so Sutter captured the tips of Kendall's nipples through her shirt, between the thumb and forefinger of each hand.

Kendall gasped, a molten river of Sutter-inspired pleasure flowing down her rib cage to meet the flickering flames of desire ignited by Josh's touch. She was intensely aware of her pants being unsnapped, of the zipper buzzing against her belly as Josh pulled it down. She felt his hands at her waist, and arched her hips as he pulled her jeans away, taking her panties off with them. Kendall reached for the hem of her sweater and pulled it off. She reached for her bra, but Sutter was there first, deftly releasing the front catch and sliding the straps down her arms. She opened her eyes briefly and looked up, catching a glimpse of him bending over the couch. He reclaimed her right breast with his hand as he kissed her roughly, his eager tongue invading her mouth. Kendall closed her eyes, sparring with Sutter's tongue while he kneaded her nipple with his thumb.

Josh's hands urged her hips closer to the edge of the couch, then spread her legs wide. Kendall moaned when Sutter pulled his mouth away. A moment later, red-hot flares erupted in her pussy as Josh's lips closed around her clit and Sutter's tongue simultaneously began teasing her nipple. "Oh, God," she murmured. Sutter's mouth enveloped the dark peak while he massaged her other nipple with his free hand. Josh pressed his lips tight to the flesh around Kendall's throbbing clit, teasing the hard nub with his tongue. "Mmmmm," Kendall moaned. They both began sucking — gently, at first. Occasionally torturing her nipple or her clit with the touch of a tongue or the sharp edge of a tooth. "Oh, God," Kendall gasped, "Yes." She spread her legs farther, flooding Josh's senses with a surge of intense desire. A deep satisfaction settled in his core, and he began sucking harder, occasionally sliding his tongue down to the edge of Kendall's vagina, tasting her salty emissions, tormenting her. Sutter moved his attentions to her other breast, taking the entire areola into his mouth, drawing the tender peak at its center deep into his throat.

The physical sensations they were inspiring took Kendall's breath away. But the real surprise came when she relaxed fully. She quit thinking about whether the situation was right or wrong and gave herself up to the moment, opening herself to the bond. A torrent of emotions flooded into her. Sutter's barely controlled primal need, punctuated by fierce joy each time Kendall gasped or cried out; Josh's more sedate, quiet delight at finally being able to touch her — to taste her — underscored by a rising tide of desire. Kendall shivered, writhing desperately as their two hungry mouths devoured her. She couldn't take it, it was too much — but then her hands were convulsing, grasping the sofa cushions with a death grip. "Yes!" she screamed. Her back arched and her body shuddered as she rode the leading edge of a white-hot fire that threatened to engulf her. Josh moved his head and thrust his tongue deep inside her pussy, savoring her sweet-tart cum, the way her cunt contracted violently on his invading tongue. He immersed himself completely in their joined consciousness, trembling in anticipation of her orgasm.

Kendall gripped the cushions, balanced precariously on the verge of fulfillment. Sutter moaned against her breast and Kendall sensed for the second time that near-painful, overwhelming pressure. Then a mixture of blissful relief and pure ecstasy flooded her limbs and she knew that Sutter's cock had exploded. And she *felt* it. "God, yes!" Kendall screamed, and tumbled into bliss, her climax merging with his, unable to distinguish where Sutter's rapture ended and hers began. Kendall thrashed violently against her lovers' mouths for several seconds, then finally collapsed, uttering a small sob, already wanting *more.*

Josh pulled himself up onto the sofa and gently pushed a sweat-soaked strand of Kendall's hair back from her temples. "Are you all right?" he murmured. Kendall nodded, though she was still trembling. Josh knew they should probably stop now, give her some time to assimilate what was happening, but he couldn't bring himself to suggest it. Sutter and Kendall had climaxed, but Josh's cock was still ripe. Full and throbbing, begging for relief. He kissed her.

Kendall's previous sexual partners had not performed cunnilingus, so she met Josh's kiss reluctantly at first, embarrassed to think that his mouth had just invaded her pussy. But her own scent, the taste of her juices on his tongue — it wasn't a turn-off, like she had imagined it would be. It was like a match, rekindling the fire in her groin. Josh reached down to his pants. He slipped out of them while he devoured Kendall with his kiss. Sutter joined them on the couch, sitting to the other side of her, breathing sweet syllables into her ear, nibbling on her neck. Josh reached for Kendall's hand and guided it to his inflamed cock, pressing her cool fingers around the hot, hard flesh.

For a moment, an unwelcome memory flashed in Kendall's mind, but she forced it away. Josh's need made her nerves hum like a tuning fork and nothing was more important to her right now than fulfilling that need.

Kendall caressed his thick shaft. As she circled the head with her fingers, a pearlescent droplet gathered at its tip. Kendall swiped the drop onto the tip of her forefinger and brought it to her lips. Smiling at Josh, she licked.

"Kendall," he groaned, leaning over to kiss her hungrily. He guided her hand back to his cock, wrapping her fingers around him, moving her up and down urgently. "Please, Kendall," he rasped. "Make me come."

Kendall shivered as Sutter lifted her hair and began tasting the back of her neck. His fingers crept over her thigh and found her clit. "Yes," she whispered. Kendall wrapped her other hand around Josh's cock. He pushed the hair back from her shoulder, kissing her neck and nibbling her ear. Kendall closed her eyes and explored Josh's manhood, relishing the frissons of pleasure that erupted through the bond as her fingers memorized the feel of him; emitting her own sensations of bliss as Sutter played with her clit.

Sutter's fingers slipped into her pussy and Kendall whimpered, her hands tightening on Josh's throbbing shaft. "Please, Kendall," he whispered, his voice shaking. Kendall opened her eyes and watched as she began pumping his cock vigorously. *Yes.* She wanted him to come—wanted to *see* his climax. Wanted to *feel* it inside her, the way she had experienced Sutter's.

Sutter had buried his face in her neck, his fingers thrusting over and over into her dripping pussy. Kendall parted her legs a little more, so that he could go deeper, and as she shifted she caught a glimpse of their reflection on the dark television screen.

It was like a bucket of ice water thrown over her. The sight of Sutter's hand disappearing beneath the quivering mound that was her stomach. Her pale, plump body between their lean, dark physiques. Her thirty-something features next to their youthful, unlined faces. *How could they possibly want me?* She tried to push the thought away, but her mind jabbered at her. *Because no one their age would do this. Because a lonely, middle-aged woman, flattered by their attentions, would be less likely to resist the idea than the slender young coeds at the college.*

Kendall pushed them both from her and stood. "I'm sorry," she stammered. She grabbed her jeans from the floor and tried to pull them on with trembling hands. Josh groaned and watched helplessly, his cock aching for release. He reached out to Kendall but she backed away.

Josh glanced at Sutter, and Sutter stood, putting his arms around Kendall as Josh grabbed his pants and yanked them on. "What's wrong?" he asked.

Kendall shook her head, pulling from his grasp. "Please, just go." Her jeans finally fastened in spite of her shaking, she searched desperately for her sweater. She spotted it half-buried between the cushions of the couch and grabbed it, yanking it over her head.

"Kendall, please," Josh implored. Kendall headed toward the front door, pulled back the deadbolt, and held the door open wide. The two of them walked toward her. Josh hesitated at the threshold, but then stepped out. Sutter stood staring at her for a long moment, then slapped his hand against the wall. "Damn it, Kendall! What is it?"

Kendall fought back tears. "This was a mistake." She met his gaze steadily, willing herself not to break down in front of them. Sutter reached out, but she backed away. "Don't—don't touch me."

His eyes searched hers.

"Please," she choked out. "Just go."

Sutter shook his head, but stepped outside. Kendall closed the door quickly and threw the deadbolt. She leaned back against the cool wood and slid to the floor, finally sobbing.

Josh and Sutter stood on the landing, listening to Kendall cry.

"What happened?" Sutter asked, bewildered. "I thought..." His voice trailed off and he shook his head.

"I felt some sort of—shock—go through the bond just before she threw us off," Josh murmured. "But I wasn't concentrating. I was more preoccupied with—you know. Did you feel it?"

"Yeah. But it was the same for me. I was just enjoying—and I thought she was, too."

"Shhh." Kendall's sobs were abating and Josh gestured for Sutter to follow him down the steps. They walked around to the car. Sutter stuck his keys in the ignition, then gripped the steering wheel and abruptly rested his head against it, groaning.

"Somehow, we blew it." He hadn't even realized how important Kendall was to him until that moment. Now, it felt as though she had been a part of them from the beginning. "And she's the one, Josh. What are we going to do?"

Josh rested a hand on his shoulder. "The main thing is not to give up." His grip tightened as he glanced toward the apartment over the shop. "We found her. We won't let her go."

Sutter turned his head and searched Josh's eyes.

"Think about it," Josh insisted. "We've been living with this bond for fourteen years, and it was something we only gradually became aware of. For her, it was instant." He shivered at the memory. "And intense. Whatever the problem is, she'll tell us. You can't turn your back on something like this."

Sutter tested the bond, and found that Josh really believed everything would turn out all right. Reassured, he started up the car and pulled out onto the street, watching as Kendall's apartment dwindled in the rearview mirror.

Chapter Three
Strange Magnetism

Kendall opened her eyes reluctantly. Her head was throbbing. She glanced at the clock on her bedside table. Eight o'clock. Two hours before she had to open up the shop. She rubbed her face and sat up. She still had on the clothes she'd worn the day before. She peeled off her sweater as she headed for the shower, then stopped as the raw throbbing of her nipples brought the events of the night before flooding back.

God. Kendall retraced her steps and sat on the edge of the bed. How could she have invited them to her home? They were just kids, really. *Kids?* her mind asked skeptically as the memory of their touch made her body ache longingly. It had been so damn *good*. Kendall shook her head. *No. It's probably just a game for them. A youthful experiment.* But that irritating voice in her head wouldn't go away. The night before, it was telling her to run away. Now, it was telling her to run back into their arms before it was too late. She wished it would make up its mind.

What about the bond? the voice chided. Yes, what about that? It was frightening to think that someone else could know her thoughts and feel what she felt. Letting someone that close gave new meaning to the word 'intimate'. At times, especially with Sutter's thoughts—so primal, so urgent—the bond had seemed like an invasion. But more often, it had been an expansion of awareness unlike anything she'd ever known before—living two lives at once. Feeling for the first time what it was like to be a man—so painfully tight, then exploding in ecstasy. Kendall drew in a shuddering breath, her body warming with the memory. She could almost understand now why men were so eager to bypass foreplay and get to the finish line. *That's right; they were enjoying themselves,* her internal voice continued. Kendall bit her lip, picturing again her less-than-perfect body writhing between them. *No, no, no,* the voice insisted. *This isn't about them, it's about you. Your insecurities. If you want to know how they really feel, it's as easy as a touch.*

It was true. Whatever else she might doubt, she couldn't deny that. The bond between them was real. Scary, but real. And she didn't think it would be possible to lie to someone through that intimate connection. *Talk to them,* the voice urged. *Give them a chance.* "But it won't work!" she wailed aloud. She was thirty-two years old. She was ready for a home. Children. Something permanent. The silent room mocked her. Kendall stood and made her way to the shower

* * * * *

She knew the moment they entered the shop. Every nerve in her body tingled. Kendall turned away from the register. When they reached the counter, she walked over and waited, twirling the pencil in her hands nervously.

"About last night," Josh began. Kendall felt heat rising in her cheeks and looked away.

"It wasn't a mistake, Kendall. You know that."

Kendall looked from him to Sutter and waited. Even without touch, she could feel how much they were hurting. "Are you sure about that?" she asked softly. The silence stretched for several minutes, until Kendall felt tears forming and blinked rapidly to keep them from falling. *How silly*, she thought. *I barely know them*. But the urge to cry wouldn't go away. *Please*, she thought. *Say something*.

"*I'll* say something," Sutter said.

Kendall's heart skipped a beat. "How did you—"

"It's easier for us," Sutter said. "We don't have to be touching. Eventually, you'll feel us even when we're hundreds of miles away. That is, if..." He glanced at Josh and stopped.

I'm scared, Kendall thought, looking into the stormy pools that were Josh's eyes. She tried to look away and couldn't. "What happened?" he asked.

Kendall saw again that reflection on the TV screen. Josh's gaze narrowed. She thrust the image aside. "I'm thirty-two years old," she said.

"So?"

Kendall moved over to a rack of fantasy bookmarks and began sorting displaced stock onto the correct hangers. "I'm ready to settle down," she said. "Get married. Maybe even start a family."

"Okay."

Kendall froze. "What did you say?"

"Okay," Josh repeated.

Kendall turned slowly to face them. "What—" She swallowed as her voice cracked, then tried again. "What does that mean?"

"Settle down with us," Josh said. "Marry us. Have children with *us*."

"You can't possibly mean that. You barely know me."

Josh shook his head. "We know you better than you know yourself."

Kendall took an involuntary step toward them. Everything in her wanted to say yes. To laugh—to cry—for joy.

"Kendall." Sutter's voice was thick with emotion. "We've been waiting for you. We love you."

"That's crazy." Kendall shook her head. "We just met!"

Sutter held out his hand. Kendall took another step, and another. When she was close enough, Sutter grasped her hand tightly, like a drowning man. "We love you," he repeated.

Kendall shook her head again. "It couldn't possibly work. I'm ten years older than you. You'll be going away to law school. I'll—" She gasped as Sutter's mind invaded hers. It was very different from the joining of the night before. This time he was probing. Searching. Pulling at her thoughts.

"Stop!" Kendall tried to tug her hand away.

"Show me."

Kendall struggled to break away. "Josh?" He stood silent, watching. Then he reached out and rested his hand on Sutter's shoulder.

"You're hurting me!"

"Show us, Kendall."

"Fine!" Angry, Kendall thrust forward the thoughts and images that had entered her mind the night before. Sutter's anger faded, and his features softened. He released his grasp and cupped her face in his hands. "How can you think that way? You're beautiful," he whispered. He kissed her passionately. "Every inch of you."

Josh leaned in and whispered in her ear. "And we're going to spend the rest of our lives making sure you believe it."

Kendall's pulse raced. She wanted to believe, but... "How can this work?" she asked.

"Just give it some time," he urged. "We'll take it slow. Get to know each other a little better. We'll find a way." His voice deepened. Husky. Seductive. Kendall gasped as her mind flooded with their admiration, desire, love. "Now that we've found you, we'll never let you go."

She closed her eyes and tried to bring to mind that image she'd built. Of herself and a quiet, sensible man; the two of them ensconced in a charming little house with two cars, two kids and a dog. Living a quiet, sensible life in a quiet, sensible neighborhood. She couldn't do it.

Sutter's hand followed the curve of her neck, his fingers slipped into the warm hollow between her breasts. He pushed aside her bra, releasing one protruding nipple. "Say yes, Kendall," he whispered.

Kendall moaned. Glancing quickly around, Sutter pulled her neckline down, exposing the dark, straining nub. Josh leaned across the counter and circled the taut peak with his tongue.

In Kendall's mind, their desire was a red tide threatening to sweep her away. "Yes," she gasped. Josh raised his head. Kendall opened her eyes as his warm, wet touch receded.

"Yes to this," he murmured, rolling her flushed nipple between a thumb and forefinger, "Or yes—to everything?"

"To everything," Kendall moaned. God, her pussy was throbbing. She considered climbing onto the counter and begging them to fuck her, right there.

Josh's eyes flashed. "Are you sure?"

Kendall nodded, no longer certain exactly what question she was answering. He looked toward the door of the shop, then came around the counter. With one powerful movement, he had lifted her onto the counter. "Lie down," he commanded.

Kendall hesitated. Anyone passing by outside could look in and see, but with her own need and their desire coursing through her veins, she found she couldn't care less. She leaned back and raised her legs. Josh pushed her skirt up over her knees. Sutter stepped forward. Kendall gasped as they slipped their fingers beneath her panties, fingering her cunt. "Oh, God," she moaned.

Rapidly, they pumped their fingers in and out. Kendall's pussy became wetter with each stroke. "God, yes!"

"That's it, Kendall." Josh glanced out the window as a car pulled into the parking lot. "Come for us, baby," he urged. "Come!"

Kendall sucked in a deep breath as her pussy spasmed, clutching at the firm fingers twisting inside her. She reached out and held them still, deep within her, back arching as her orgasm peaked.

They removed their fingers and Josh lifted her to the floor as the bell over the door jangled, retaining his grip on her waist until her panting subsided and her rubbery legs would support her. He stepped out from behind the counter and Kendall turned to face them, her cheeks warm.

Sutter brought his fingers to his nose and inhaled deeply, bringing an even deeper rose flush to Kendall's cheeks. She glanced behind him, making sure her customers hadn't noticed. "Can we see you tonight?" he asked.

Kendall nodded.

"When do you close?"

Kendall swallowed. She seemed to be having difficulty finding her voice. "Eight o'clock," she finally said.

"We'll be back to pick you up at eight-thirty."

Kendall smiled and nodded as a couple walked up and began studying the jewelry display. Stepping out from behind the counter, she gestured for Sutter and Josh to follow her to the door. "What should I wear?" she asked.

"We own a beach house," Sutter offered. "It's very private. We could have a bonfire." He allowed his gaze to travel hungrily over Kendall's body, then grinned wickedly. "Maybe do a little skinny-dipping."

Kendall's nipples tightened abruptly. "That sounds— very nice," she agreed, rather breathlessly.

Sutter leaned in and kissed her goodbye, flooding her senses with his desire until her knees turned to putty. When the bell over the door jangled again, Kendall pushed him away. "Go!" she ordered.

Her two lovers reluctantly moved away. "Oh, and pack a bag," Sutter suggested just before the door swung shut behind them.

Chapter Four
Taking the Plunge

Kendall locked the doors precisely at eight and rushed up to her apartment to change. She slipped into jeans and a loose t-shirt and stared at herself in the mirror. *Hair up or down?* At first, she was leaning toward wearing it loose, but finally pinned it up in a curly mass on her head. She thought for a moment, then grabbed a canvas bag and tucked in a nightgown and clothes for the next day. Then she went over to the dresser and opened a drawer, staring down at her navy-blue, one-piece skirted swimsuit. Josh had said they'd be skinny-dipping, but Kendall couldn't picture herself naked in front of them. Pulling it out, she walked over to the mirror and held it before her. *Yuck*, she thought. *This is NOT how I want them to see me.*

Sudden inspiration hit, and she went back to the dresser, digging in the bottom drawer until she came up with the gift her friends had given her a few years back, when they were trying to convince her to broaden her horizons a bit—live a little dangerously. It was still in the box. A nightshirt made completely of loose-woven white lace. She pulled it out and slipped it over her head. The lacy confection softened her silhouette and made her appear slimmer. It might be a little chilly on the beach, but there would be a fire, and it was still early November. Temperatures for the last few days had been in the low eighties.

Kendall smiled at herself in the mirror, then pulled off the shirt and slipped it into her bag. Turning, she stepped into her sandals, then went into the bathroom and snagged her toothbrush and toothpaste. She thought about putting on more makeup, but decided against it. In the fall and winter, she usually wore mascara and a touch of blush; in the summer, mascara and a light pink, frosted lipstick that looked good with her tan, but other than that she rarely wore a lot of makeup. She would just be herself. Fortunately, Josh and Sutter seemed more than willing to accept her as she was. The doorbell rang, and Kendall grabbed her bag and purse and headed into the living room.

"Hi!" Kendall smiled and stepped outside, turning back to lock the door. At the sight of her jeans stretched tight and smooth across her buttocks, Josh's cock immediately began to swell. He had never received any relief the night before, and it had been hours before his erection finally subsided. The sudden rush of blood to his penis was surprisingly painful. Josh put his arms around her waist and kissed the back of her neck. He wanted to rub his throbbing cock against her, but was still concerned about what had happened the previous night, and decided not to push it. Besides, as aroused as he was, he was likely to shoot his load right away, and that would definitely spoil the fun. Kendall dropped her keys into her purse and turned, kissing him lightly on the cheek. He took her hand and they jogged down the steps and around to the front, where Sutter was waiting in the car.

The three of them made small talk during the forty-five minutes it took to reach their destination. Sutter finally pulled off the highway onto a winding dirt road that led to a house perched on a rocky promontory. He pulled into the drive and cut the engine.

"Wow!" Kendall stepped out of the car, awed. The house was built sort of like a log cabin but with logs more slender than was traditional, and on a huge scale. They walked up the steps to the front porch. Carved into a half-medallion above the front door were a handful of cavorting dolphins, polished to the point where they glimmered in the moonlight. Kendall noticed similar adornments above the windows, and mermaids ornamented the shutters flanking them. "These are beautiful," she breathed.

"Josh designed it," Sutter offered.

Josh smiled. "But Sutter's the artist. He did the carvings."

"My God! Really?" Kendall asked. "These are fantastic! I didn't know you were an artist."

Sutter seemed uncomfortable. "I'm not."

Josh frowned and started to speak, but then shook his head and unlocked the front door, ushering Kendall inside.

Highly polished wood gleamed everywhere. A dark stain on the logs that made up the wall of the living room to her right served as an effective backdrop for pieces of furniture fashioned of a lighter-colored wood. An unusual fur rug—nearly black, with silvery strands interspersed—covered the floor in front of a fireplace which was faced in natural stones. A low dividing wall stood between the living area and the den beyond which contained a pool table and recliner at one end, a big-screen television and stereo system fronted by a comfortable-looking overstuffed couch at the other end. A wall of windows offered a stunning view of the gulf.

"This place is beautiful."

Josh shrugged as though it wasn't important, but appeared very pleased.

"Can I put those up for you?" Sutter asked, reaching for her purse and bag.

"Well, are we still going down to the beach?"

Sutter nodded.

"Then I guess I should change first."

Sutter showed her to the bathroom. "We'll wait for you on the deck out back." Kendall nodded, shutting the door behind her. She sat on the side of the tub, her heart pounding. Quickly, before she had time to see herself in the mirror and change her mind, she slipped out of her clothes and pulled the lace shirt over her head. She closed her eyes for a moment and took a deep breath, then pulled open the door and stepped out.

As she entered the pool room, a light breeze wafted into the house from the door that now stood open onto the deck. Sutter and Josh were sitting at a picnic table outside, talking in low tones. Kendall stepped out into the night. Sutter glanced over and uttered a long, low whistle. Kendall blushed and looked away.

Josh swallowed hard. The breeze teased at Kendall's lace cover-up, conforming it to her generous curves. Beneath the lace, her skin was bare, gleaming in the moonlight.

Sutter and Josh exchanged glances. "To the beach?" Sutter asked.

"Definitely."

"Kendall?" She nodded. Sutter grabbed a lantern, lighter fluid and a box of fireplace matches from the top of the picnic table, and led the way down a meandering set of steps that ended at the beach.

There was a pile of wood already assembled there. Sutter squirted some lighter fluid onto the lower branches and lit several matches, throwing them into the heap. In a few short minutes, he had a nice fire burning.

Josh had spread out a blanket on the sand a little way from the fire and was sitting there, watching Kendall. She walked over and settled onto the ground beside him. Sutter joined them, and there was an awkward silence. They sat staring at each other for several minutes, until Kendall finally laughed.

"What's so funny?" Sutter asked.

"The two of you," she said. Her eyes danced with humor. "You were so bold when you *didn't* have me." She leaned back on her arms, flickering firelight offering the briefest glimpses of her bare skin beneath the lace. "Don't you know what to do with me now that you do?"

Sutter's eyes glinted in the glow from the fire. Josh hesitated, but then both he and Sutter were moving forward, pushing Kendall back against the blanket. They ran their hands over the curves of her breasts, the mound of her tummy, down along her thighs. Again and again, over the lace. Sultry heat invaded Kendall's limbs, whipped into eddies of desperate longing until she was breathless with the desire to feel their flesh against hers. "Josh," she whispered. He reached out and cupped one of her breasts in his hand, his skin tantalizingly warm against the bits of flesh exposed through the lacy mesh.

Josh bent and covered her nipple with his mouth, teasing the bits of skin that showed through the lace with his tongue. Kendall moaned and reached up, tangling the fingers of one hand in his curly hair. With the other, she reached out and grasped one of Sutter's hands, bringing it to her other breast. She held it there while he kneaded her. After a moment, he turned his hand over and grabbed her fingers, pressing them against her breast. In the flickering firelight, he watched her with hungry eyes. "Play with it for me," he whispered.

Josh raised his head and waited, eyes glued to her hand. Kendall took a deep, shaky breath and began running her fingers over her sensitive nipple. "Mmmm," Josh murmured, closing his mouth over her breast again, but keeping his face angled so that he could watch.

Kendall sensed their rising excitement and felt a delightful tingle in her crotch. She parted her legs and, making sure she had their attention, slowly trailed her hand down to her pussy, dipping her middle finger into her vagina and drawing it back up to her nipple. Her juices glimmered on the bare skin visible beneath the lace. "Baby," Sutter whispered. He rolled up the hem of her shirt, Josh relinquishing her nipple just long enough for Sutter to pull the cover-up over her head. Josh resumed sucking and watched as Kendall reached for her crotch again, then continued to lubricate the other nipple. Wetting it, pinching it, rolling the hard nub between her fingers. Sutter observed avidly, until finally he groaned and bent over, taking her finger in his mouth, alternately sucking her juices from the long digit and the hard peak beneath.

Kendall gasped. It was breathtaking, having both her breasts sucked at the same time, and in such different ways. Josh's touch was soft, his lips gentle, his tongue teasing her lightly, sending ripples of excitement down to her abdomen. Sutter's mouth *demanded*, his lips milking her fiercely, his teeth nipping at her ripe bud and setting off explosions of desire in her crotch.

Kendall ran her fingers through their hair. Josh moaned as she tickled his ear with her fingertip. He moved, supporting himself on his elbow as he stretched out beside her. Watching her closely, he traced curlicues on her tummy as Sutter raised his head and began sucking on the nipple Josh had vacated. "Mmmm," Kendall murmured. She raised up onto her elbows, watching Josh's face as he trailed his fingers through her bush, playing with the dark curls. Kendall spread her legs wide.

Josh circled her clit with his thumb. "Josh," Kendall whispered. He pressed his thumb tightly against the nub, massaging gently. "Yes, Josh," Kendall moaned.

Sutter raised himself, turning his head so that he could see her crotch. Fireworks exploded in his groin at the sight of Kendall's swollen clit beneath Josh's thumb. He reached out a hand, glancing significantly up at Josh as he did so. Josh understood, and together they slipped their forefingers into Kendall's glistening cunt while Josh continued to rub her clitoris in lazy circles. "Oh, God!" Kendall arched her back. Sutter bent again to her nipple, drawing the tip, chilled by the night air, eagerly back into his warm, welcoming mouth. Kendall shuddered. This was heaven—Sutter's mouth on her breast, Josh's thumb rubbing her clitoris. And *both their fingers* inside her, moving independently of each other—Josh's touch gentle and languorous, massaging the walls of her vagina, making his way slowly around the perimeter; Sutter's finger eager and aggressive in comparison, plunging in and out, rapid and deep.

Kendall wanted to feel their cocks. Sutter chuckled as he read her thought and swung around so that she could reach him. "Here, let me help." He pushed his swimsuit down over his hips. Kendall watched her hand close over his long, rigid member. Josh took his finger from her crotch, and Kendall moaned. He grinned as he rearranged himself as well, pulling off his suit and guiding her other hand to his own cock. His eyes closed as her cool fingers wrapped around his inflamed flesh. He reached back toward her pussy. "Come for us again, baby. Like you did in the store," he said as he slipped his finger back inside her. "We love watching you come." Kendall arched. Her vaginal wall spasmed as Josh massaged a little more roughly this time, as Sutter's finger lunged into her over and over.

Sutter leaned over, compressing Kendall's clit between his lips. "Oh, God." Kendall's voice shook. "Yes." She began running her hands up and down the lengths of their stiff shafts, holding them tight.

"Wait," Josh murmured. Sutter raised his head and watched as Josh dipped two fingers into Kendall's pussy, cupping them as he dragged them out, then rubbing the captured juices all over his cock. Sutter followed suit, reaching deep inside her, harvesting more of the thick liquid and then lubricating his own erection. Kendall began milking them again, slowly at first, then faster and faster. Josh and Sutter were sitting up now, watching. In unison, they plunged their forefingers into her pussy again and again, fucking her gently at first, then more and more vigorously as they themselves came closer to orgasm.

Kendall closed her eyes, searching for the sense of them, for their thoughts and feelings in the torrent of sensation roaring through her. A wave of powerful, carnal need washed over her—Sutter. She tightened her hand on his cock. He reached down with his free hand and pressed her fingers into his flesh, holding her tight against him. "Faster," he urged, and Kendall obliged.

Josh was a barely restrained pressure, building behind a dam inside her, tightly controlled. Kendall smiled. She didn't want him under control—she wanted him wild. Desperate. She tilted his swollen member toward her gently, urging him to scoot up closer to her head. When he was near enough, she half-turned and wrapped her lips around his broad, bulging manhood.

Strung tight with unrelieved need since the night before, Josh gasped. With the warm mouth that had haunted his dreams finally touching his flesh, he couldn't hold back. He exploded. Kendall felt him spurting into her just as Sutter's semen fountained onto her hand. She pressed her lips tight around Josh's pulsing flesh and drank every drop. He shuddered, pushing her head down, burying the tip of his cock in her throat. He plunged another finger into her quivering pussy.

Kendall whimpered deep in her throat as her orgasm peaked. Josh and Sutter groaned simultaneously, all three of them bucking and writhing on the blanket. As the final pulse of their penises faded and Kendall's strong contractions abated, Josh sighed with contentment. Kendall swallowed the last of his cum and lay back on the blanket. He removed his fingers from her pussy and lay beside her. Kendall turned her head and kissed him, her lips soft against his. He could taste himself on her mouth, and it was good.

Sutter withdrew his own finger and sat where he was, panting. Kendall patted the blanket near her head. He moved up and she turned toward him. She began darting her tongue in and out of her mouth, lapping up the semen sprinkled over his thighs, his abdomen. Sutter groaned and wrapped his hand around her head as blood rushed again to his penis.

Kendall saved his cock for last, experiencing deep satisfaction as she drew her tongue over its tip, noting he was already plump and standing at attention again. She sat up. "I want one of you inside me," she demanded. She turned to Josh. "Now."

Sutter looked at Josh. "In the water?" he asked. Josh nodded. Sutter picked Kendall up and carried her into the waves. Kendall shuddered. The gulf waters were warm, but the cool night air raised goosebumps on her skin. Sutter carried her out into the gulf until the waters swirled around his waist.

Josh joined them. Sutter set Kendall on her feet, and they wrapped their arms around her, sandwiching her between them. Kendall pressed her nipples into Sutter's chest, and wiggled her hips. Sutter was quite a bit taller than her—his cock rolled back and forth between her upper abdomen and his pelvis, the tip of it just grazing the bottom of her breasts. Josh was closer to her own height, so his cock nestled tightly against her back, between the upper swells of her butt cheeks.

Kendall sighed and relaxed between her lovers. Through their empathic connection surges of delight, anticipation and longing were sweeping into her from them, permeating her being. *This is exactly where I belong*, Kendall thought to herself. She felt a rush of pleasure from Josh and Sutter, and knew that they could feel her contentment. The three of them remained that way for a long while, sifting through the mix of emotions, reveling in their knowledge of each other.

Eventually, Sutter drew back, turning Kendall insistently to face Josh. Kendall shivered in anticipation. It had been a long while since she last had sex and her pussy ached to be filled. Sutter reached over her shoulders from behind and grabbed her waist. She reached up and held on to his biceps. Josh stood in front of her, memorizing the sight of her bare breasts limned by the moonlight, glistening with sea-spray.

"Fuck me, Josh," Kendall whispered urgently. Josh groaned, and Sutter lifted her from the sea floor. Josh pulled her hips forward, so that she was lying back against Sutter's stomach, supported by his strong arms. Josh guided his cock to the mouth of her tight pussy, pressing against the opening. Kendall watched eagerly. Josh pushed into her.

Kendall gasped as his engorged head squeezed past her vaginal opening. "So *thick*," she murmured. The sight of her watching him avidly, eagerly, flooded Josh's groin with raw heat. He longed to stuff himself inside her, but he wanted to prolong the experience. Savor it. He eased in a little farther.

Kendall winced and tensed abruptly. After such a long period of sexual inactivity, her pussy was extremely tight, and Josh had the thickest cock she'd ever seen, stretching her painfully. "I'm sorry," she breathed. "You're just so big."

"It's okay," he murmured. He lifted Kendall's legs until they were wrapped around him, holding his prick steady about one-third of the way inside her. Then he reached out and cupped both her breasts in his hands.

Kendall moaned as he massaged the flushed buds between his thumbs and forefingers. Sutter shifted his grip on her waist. While Josh held her left nipple tightly between his thumb and forefinger, pinching, making the hard little nub stand out, Sutter leaned over and tickled its tip with his tongue. "Oh, God," Kendall moaned. He wiggled his tongue faster. "God, yes!"

Josh inched his cock a little farther into her pussy. Kendall moaned, trying desperately to relax her vaginal muscles so that she could take all of him. "Fuck me," she demanded. The feel of him was so good, she couldn't keep her pussy from contracting involuntarily against his firm flesh. Josh felt her tightening around his cock, and barely resisted the urge to plunge into her. Instead, he squeezed her captured nipples, pulling the two peaks toward each other.

Sutter's tongue danced back and forth between Kendall's swollen nubs, coaxing tiny cries of pleasure from deep in her throat. He tightened the grip of his one hand on her waist and reached between her legs with the other, trapping her throbbing clit between his fingers. He squeezed the tiny bud the same way Josh was squeezing her nipples. Kendall felt the blood rushing into her groin. "Oh, please, please," she moaned. "Fuck me."

Josh inched his prick back slightly. "No!" Kendall protested. The flame of her need licked along his veins. He let go of her nipples and pressed her huge breasts tight together, until the dark tips were touching. Sutter covered them both with his mouth and began sucking, milking her breasts with his lips and her clit with his fingers. "Oh God, please," Kendall sobbed. "Please!" She could feel their emotions dancing through the bond. They were playing with her, teasing her. Wanted her frantic when they finally gave her what she needed.

Though the small cove they were in was somewhat protected from the surf by the promontory, small waves broke over Kendall as her two young lovers brought her closer and closer to the point of no return. When a particularly vigorous wave nudged them and caused Josh's cock to slip slightly within her, it was more than she could take. She let go of Sutter's arms and reached for Josh, wanting to grasp his shoulders and ram her pussy down onto his shaft.

But Sutter's hand held her waist in a death grip, and she couldn't reach Josh. She moaned and arched desperately.

"What do you want?" Josh teased.

"Fuck me," Kendall begged.

"This?" Josh pressed into her, his cock sliding a fraction of an inch farther toward her core.

Kendall no longer felt any pain — nothing save intense, desperate need. "Yes," she moaned. "Please, yes."

"And this?" he slid in farther.

"Oh God, Josh," she groaned. "Please. All of it!" She arched her back again, and Josh grabbed her hips and drove his cock into the heart of her warmth.

"Yes!" Kendall screamed. *Yes.* As fine as they felt, fingers were no substitute for a ripe, throbbing cock. And his was so thick. He filled her completely, every part of her pulsating flesh pressed tight against his hot, steely rod. Sutter milked her clit vigorously. Josh pounded himself into her — big, so *big* — and Kendall bucked frantically, loving the feel of it. Her pussy ached, stretched firmly around him. Kendall fought to breathe as waves of ecstasy pummeled her body. She could feel it *all*. Her own excitement, the roiling rush that was Josh's impending release. Sutter's frank enjoyment at watching their arousal, coupled with the humming approach of his own, milder orgasm. She grasped Josh tightly with her legs, grinding her pelvis into his. She closed her eyes and saw herself and Josh as Sutter saw them — excited by their pleasure, thrilled by her presence. Thinking how beautiful she was.

Josh's entire body filled with a sultry heat as Kendall's sensations invaded the link. He felt for the first time how much she relished having a pussy full of cock. How she welcomed his hard, hot flesh. How she craved to take him even deeper. Josh plunged himself into her one last time, burying the length of his cock as deep as she could take it, and felt Kendall shudder. Sutter felt it too; and how his relentless hand on Kendall's clit was driving her crazy, and how a hungry part of her was wishing she could take *both* of them inside her. His quiet arousal swelled to massive proportions at the thought. Kendall's shudders transformed into violent trembling and the ecstasy of her satisfaction hit her lovers like a tsunami. Josh and Sutter fought to remain upright as their cocks simultaneously erupted, gasping as they were sucked into a vortex of intense gratification — drowning in passion, their strength ebbing in the face of a climax the likes of which neither one had ever experienced before. Kendall threw back her head and screamed their names as her body seemed to explode and reform a million times between bursts of pure pleasure.

When it was over, Kendall went limp. Josh's knees buckled and a wave pushed Sutter's legs from beneath him. They all tumbled into the surf. Kendall came up spluttering. She gained her feet first and helped Josh and

Sutter to stand, then they made their exhausted way up onto the beach and collapsed on the sand.

"I never *imagined* it would be so good," Kendall murmured.

"Neither did we," her two lovers answered together, and Kendall smiled in satisfaction. The three of them lay in silent recuperation until Kendall's teeth started chattering. "Shouldn't we go inside?" she prompted. The guys groaned, but struggled to their feet and lifted Kendall onto hers. Sutter grabbed the blanket and their clothes and held the lantern so that they could find their way back up the stairs in the dark.

Chapter Five
Foundation

Once inside the house, Kendall started for the bathroom. "Where are you going?" Josh asked.

Kendall looked at the floor, the ceiling, the pictures on the wall—everywhere, trying to avoid staring at Josh and Sutter's nude bodies. Down on the beach, she had been totally immersed in what they were doing to her and firelight wasn't all that illuminating anyway. Here in the house, with the lights on, she could see that both their bodies were near-perfect. Tan and extremely muscular—even more attractive without clothes than she had imagined. It made her more conscious than ever of her rounded tummy and wide hips. "I was going to go put on some clothes."

Josh stepped toward her and tilted her face up to his. Gazing deep into her eyes, he caressed one of her breasts with his calloused hands. "Don't," he said.

Sutter came over and stood behind Kendall. He reached around and stroked her stomach with his hands. "Is *this* what bothers you?" Kendall half-nodded, and he whispered in her ear. "Mmmm. I'm going to rub my dick all over it; and if you'll let me, I'm going to come, and then I'm going to lick every drop from you." Kendall's heart started to gallop and she felt sultry heat flowing from his hands against her skin up into her breasts and down toward her groin.

"We love you," Josh whispered, taking her face in his hands. "Everything about you. Remember that." He kissed her, enjoying the salty, earthy taste of the sea on her lips. "Why don't you and Sutter wait in the den for me, and I'll make some hot chocolate?"

Kendall nodded, and Josh went into the kitchen while Sutter took her by the hand and drew her into the living room. He snagged a few pillows from the couch and tossed them onto the fur rug covering the floor before the fireplace. Kendall settled onto the rug Indian-style, while Sutter got the small fire going. Josh returned with their drinks, and the three of them sat on the floor warming themselves, sipping the hot cocoa.

Kendall appeared pensive, staring into the bright flames. "What are you thinking?" Josh asked.

She looked up and smiled ruefully. "Oh, how funny life can be."

"Is something wrong?"

Kendall frowned slightly. "Not exactly." She toyed with her cup, running the tip of her finger around the rim. "You have to understand — it's been a strange life. All of my relationships have been — a little weird." She met his gaze squarely. "To be perfectly honest, the only thing I've wanted for the last few years was to find a quiet, responsible type to settle down with. Someone I could trust not to hurt me. A life that would be totally uneventful, maybe even boring. I thought boring might be a nice change of pace."

The two of them looked so puzzled and worried. Kendall set her empty cup aside and curled up on the rug, her head in Josh's lap, striving to project through the bond that everything would be okay. Josh began pulling the pins from her hair, running his fingers through the tangled locks. Sutter stretched out on his side, head propped up on one arm.

"My mother was born here in the states." Kendall reached out, tracing lazy circles on Sutter's chest. "My mom was American, my dad was Irish," she explained. "They met when my dad came to visit New York on business. Anyway, she ended up marrying him and moving to Ireland. That's where I was born." Kendall closed her eyes and savored the sensation of Josh's strong fingers combing out her hair. "Up until I was five, I absolutely adored my dad. But around then, I started noticing that my mother cried nearly every night. Sometimes I would hear loud voices and strange noises, and the next morning she would be covered in bruises. Of course, he was beating her. But I didn't realize it at first. I was convinced that a monster was sneaking into our house at night and hurting her, and I didn't understand why my dad couldn't protect her."

She let out a heartfelt sigh. "Then, one day when he stayed home from work, he got mad at her and started hitting her in front of me. In our living room. I was six years old. I was screaming at him to stop, and he wouldn't, so I ran up and grabbed his arm. Without even thinking, he just threw me. Slung his arm out and threw me right across the room, through a plate-glass window."

"Damn." Sutter reached out and took Kendall's hand in his. Kendall offered him a sad smile.

"They took me to the emergency room — told the doctor I was climbing on the back of the couch and fell through the window. I don't think he bought it, but it was a small community, where they feel that a man's business is a man's business and no one else's.

"I was lucky. It wasn't that bad. I had a gash on my scalp that needed about five stitches and a few cuts on my arms, but nothing too serious. The next day, while my father was at work, my mom packed up my clothes and stuck me in the truck and drove me to her sister-in-law's house. A few days later, I was on a plane to Connecticut to live with my mother's parents." Kendall stared into the dancing flames for a few moments. "I lived with them for five years. I never did understand why my mother stayed behind, but at least she tried to protect me." She frowned slightly.

"It took a while for me to feel comfortable with my grandparents, since I had never met them before. But eventually I became very close to my grandfather. He loved the land. He used to take me on these long nature walks. He knew the names of every tree, could identify every plant by the shape of its leaves. He would hunt out snakes, spiders, lizards—taught me not to be afraid of them."

Sutter's palm was warm against hers, and Kendall rubbed the back of his hand with her thumb. "Then when I was eleven, we went on a nature hike one day, just like usual. We stopped under this huge white oak. We sat down and rested for a few minutes and then he turned to me and I thought he was going to say something, but he put his arm around me and kissed me on the lips, and stuck his tongue in my mouth."

Kendall felt them tense, and felt their outrage flowing through her. She was grateful. "I was *shocked*. I'd never French-kissed a boy before, but I knew what it was. I didn't even pull away, I was so confused. I couldn't believe he was doing that. Then he..." she faltered, and Josh whispered, "You don't have to tell us."

Kendall nodded. "Yes, I do. I want you to know. He reached inside the waistband of my pants and — touched me, under my panties. I said 'no', and tried to pull his hand out, but he said he just wanted to show me how much he loved me. He said 'I just want you to know that none of those boys you go to school with are ever going to love you the way I do.' Then he tried to kiss me again."

"Damn it!" Sutter exclaimed. He was so angry his hand shook, but Kendall's emotions through the bond were calm. Sad, but without anger. He couldn't believe it.

"I dealt with all this a long time ago, Sutter, but I wanted the two of you to understand why the decision to become involved in such a — unique — relationship was a hard one for me to make."

He nodded, and she continued.

"I pushed him, hard, and then got up and ran. When I got to the house, I ran into my bedroom and locked the door and called my mom. The worst thing about the whole experience was — my mom knew he was like that. When I told her what he had done, she said 'He promised me he wouldn't touch you.' I couldn't believe it. She sent me to live with him, knowing he was like that. He had done it to her as a child. Maybe that explains why she put up with my dad.

"Anyway, my grandfather came home and yelled at me through the door, pounding on it, telling me he was only showing me what love really meant. My mom stayed on the phone with me until my grandmother came home, then had me let her in and put her on the phone. The upshot was that I ended up moving to Texas to live with my half-brother. Basically, at that point I felt like everyone I had ever loved had betrayed me."

Josh brushed her cheek with his fingers. "My God," he said, "I'm so sorry."

Kendall smiled up at him. "But you see, this is why you can never wish to go back and relive your life. If things hadn't happened the way they did, I might never have ended up with my brother. And he was the best thing that ever happened to me."

She reached up and cupped Josh's hand with hers, caressing his palm with her cheek. "Brian was Mom's son from a previous marriage. He was seventeen years older than me, never been married. He was an architect, Josh, like you. He didn't have to take me in, but he did. He's the one who taught me to make my own happiness. I could have wallowed in all the horrible things that had happened, but he wouldn't let me. He kept saying we are all exactly what we *want* to be, so if I wanted to be happy, I had to *make* it happen.

Kendall looked into Sutter's warm brown eyes. "Brian stood behind me one hundred percent in everything I ever tried to do. He taught me to trust myself, no matter what."

"You speak as though he's gone."

Kendall nodded. "Yes. He died in a plane crash a couple of years ago. And I have to admit after he was gone I started feeling a little defeated. Started thinking maybe I should just take the easy way out. Settle down with a guy I didn't really have any strong feelings for so that I couldn't be hurt. Build a quiet, calm life where I wouldn't have to face any risks." She smiled again, and the sense of happiness swirling through the bond settled comfortably in Josh and Sutter's hearts. "My head—my head can't make up its mind whether this is right or wrong. But my brother taught me to listen to my heart, and my heart says *yes.*" She squeezed Sutter's hand tight. "So, here I am. And I wouldn't change a thing."

Sutter and Josh swallowed past the lumps in their throats. Wordlessly, they lay to either side of her and wrapped her in a gentle embrace, unable to believe how amazingly lucky they were to have been drawn to such an incredible woman. As Sutter pulled a blanket from the couch and settled it over them, Kendall felt as though the three of them were the calm eye at the center of the hurricane that was life. Feeling totally secure for the first time since her brother had died, she allowed herself to drift off to sleep.

Chapter Six
Taking Charge

Kendall awoke in the morning to find them propped up on their elbows, their dark brown and silvery-grey gazes watching her. Kendall smiled and stretched like a contented cat. "Good morning," she murmured throatily.

They both grinned. "Good morning," they answered in unison. "Is everything okay?" Josh added.

Apparently, they were worried about her reaction to this relationship in the bright light of day. She sat up, letting the blanket fall to her waist. She kissed each of them in turn. Deeply. Lingeringly. "Everything's perfect."

Sutter yawned and stretched. "I don't know about you guys, but I need a shower."

"We all do," Kendall said.

Josh and Sutter stood and held out their hands to help her up. "Your wish is our command," Sutter quipped. Kendall laughed and went to grab her things, then let them lead her up the stairs, across the bedroom and into the bathroom. Sutter turned on the water and adjusted the temperature while Josh appropriated towels from the cupboard under the sink.

The shower was utterly enjoyable. Kendall eschewed the washcloth and soaped each of their bodies with her hands, gliding over their hard abdomens, memorizing the swell of their biceps, their strong, muscular thighs; relishing the way the muscles in their stomachs tightened as she knelt in front of them and ran her fingers down their penises and up between the cheeks of their butts.

Her lovers did the same for her. Sutter stood behind her and lifted her breasts, while Josh cleaned the curve where her breasts joined her abdomen with soft, sensuous strokes. Kendall found it unexpectedly erotic, and Josh grinned knowingly when her nipples hardened and protruded. Sutter knelt and soaped her belly, smiling up at her as he tickled her belly button. Then he lifted her belly as well, his soapy fingers stroking the sensitive skin just below her abdomen and above her bush. Kendall moaned softly as warmth suffused her groin.

They showered until the water started running cold. Sutter and Josh fondling Kendall's breasts, massaging her buttocks; Kendall tracing their cocks with the tips of her erect nipples, occasionally teasing them with a quick swipe of her tongue — tempting each other, but not acting on it.

Kendall slipped out while Sutter and Josh were rinsing shampoo from their hair. She dried off quickly, then wrapped her hair in the towel and went into the bedroom. Her overnight bag was on the floor beside the bed. She rummaged inside and pulled out her shirt and shorts. She had chosen a loose-fitting, low-cut peasant blouse made of an almost sheer silky material and a pair of comfortable walking shorts with roomy legs. She pulled out her undergarments, then hesitated. Smiling to herself, she put them back in the bag. She pulled the blouse over her head and reached for the shorts.

When Josh exited the bathroom, Kendall's back was turned to him and she was reaching to zip up her shorts. Josh walked over. "Let me help," he whispered in her ear. He walked around, facing her. Reaching down, he found the zipper. Her bush tickled the tips of his fingers and he held her gaze while he ran his hand down inside her pants, through the soft curls. He raised his eyebrows when he discovered she was not wearing any panties, sudden desire flashing in his eyes. His knuckles kneaded her tummy as he pulled the zipper up and fastened the snap. Slipping his hands under her shirt, he ran them up her back. He smiled and nodded when he discovered she was not wearing a bra, either. "Very nice. We're going to like this," he whispered hoarsely. He kissed her lips lightly, grasping her sides under the shirt, teasing her nipples delicately with the tips of his thumbs. Then he turned and went over to the dresser.

Sutter came in and sat on the bed, drying his hair vigorously with a towel. Kendall stood awkwardly beside the bed, unsure whether she should wait for them or head downstairs. Josh finished dressing and sauntered over to the bed, whispered in Sutter's ear, then winked at Kendall as he headed out the door.

"Come here," Sutter said. Kendall stepped closer to the bed. While they kissed, she felt his hand on the back of her thigh. It traveled upward, beneath the loose fabric, caressing her naked buttock. "Mmmm," he murmured against her lips. He turned her head and whispered in her ear. "We're going to drive you wild," he promised. Kendall reached out to stroke his naked cock, but he grabbed her hand. Kendall frowned. "We're going to stroke you," he continued, caressing her hips under the fabric, "every chance we get." He lifted her shirt and rasped the tip of his tongue across one swollen nipple. "Taste you." His eyes were nearly black with desire as he let the shirt drop, hiding her once more. He continued, his voice thick. "Make you come, over and over." Kendall felt herself trembling at the erotic promise. "Until you *beg* for it."

Kendall's eyes glittered provocatively. "Promise?" she asked, her voice thick with desire.

Sutter nodded. "All weekend long."

Kendall was breathing hard. Sutter's gaze strayed to her shirt. Her dark areoles were tempting shadows beneath the thin fabric. He swallowed past the lump of desire forming in his throat. Kendall tugged on the bottom of her shirt, pulling the neckline down until her nipples were exposed. Groaning, Sutter leaned forward and captured one brown nub between his lips. Kendall stared into his eyes, frank lust evident in her gaze.

Sutter's cock throbbed painfully, and he almost dragged her onto the bed, but he wanted to wait. They had all day, and Josh needed to be there. He released her nipple and gave her a little slap on the rump. "Go on, now. I need to get dressed."

Kendall backed away, eyeing his erection possessively, licking her lips suggestively even as she restored her neckline to its proper place. Sutter groaned and threw the towel at her. "Go on!" Kendall laughed and turned away.

Josh was standing at the stove, flipping bacon. Kendall had a strong urge to go over and caress his cock through the tight fabric of his jean shorts, but quelled it. After all, she should be getting to know them in *other* ways—and there wasn't much opportunity for conversation when they were making love. Instead, she walked over to the refrigerator and peeked in. Grabbing a jug of orange juice, she turned and set it on the counter. "The glasses are over there," Josh said, pointing with the spatula. Kendall took out three glasses, tossed in some ice and filled them; then carried them over to the table and sat, watching him cook.

Sutter came up behind her and began massaging her shoulders. "Mmmm," Kendall murmured, leaning into his touch. "You know," he whispered in her ear, "You had a pretty good idea up there." He bent over and grasped the hem of her shirt, tugging until the elastic neckline was under her breasts, once again revealing her full, ripe orbs. "That's better," he murmured. A thrill shot down Kendall's spine as she waited for him to touch them, but he returned to rubbing her shoulders. She tilted her head back and found him watching her nipples as they danced, rising and falling with each delicious squeeze. She closed her eyes. A moment later, something warm and slightly rough was scratching across the taut peaks. Kendall opened her eyes to find Josh beside her, the tantalizing touch that of the ends of two crisp strips of bacon. She wriggled and arched her back, making her breasts stand out even more. Josh held one piece of bacon up to her mouth, and she took a bite while Josh licked bacon grease from her prominent bud. He continued licking and sucking her until she had eaten the entire slice. Then, he handed Sutter the other strip and Sutter, likewise, fed her, cleaning the other nipple while she ate.

Kendall moaned and writhed in her chair. Sutter looked up at her. "What is it, baby?" Kendall stared at him in mute appeal. "Tell me," he demanded.

"I'm so horny," she whispered.

"Do you need to come?" She nodded. Sutter motioned Josh back to her side, and they each flicked their tongues across her hard, dark buds. Kendall moaned. Sutter moved his head, joining Josh on her right breast. Inadvertently, their tongues touched, and a quicksilver shiver of arousal raced down Sutter's spine. Repressing it, he drew away and returned his attention to her left breast.

Kendall clutched their shoulders. "Please," she urged. "Suck me." In silent agreement, they stuffed themselves with her malleable flesh, taking as much of each breast into their mouths as they could.

Kendall gasped. Each of their large mouths seemed to envelop nearly half a breast, and Sutter was sucking *hard*, making her tingle with mingled pain and pleasure. Josh was doing something wonderful with the back of his tongue, pressing her nipple up against the roof of his mouth as he sucked, then releasing, then pressing, then releasing. Kendall groaned and reached inside her pants waist, intending to touch herself. "No." Josh grabbed her arm and pulled out her hand. "Don't worry, baby. You'll come," he promised. He pushed her right breast over toward her left. Sutter realized what he was doing and did the same. When her nipples were nearly touching, their tongues danced randomly over both. Experimentally, Sutter allowed his tongue to contact Josh's briefly. Another electric current passed between them. Eyes wide, Josh met his gaze. In all the years they had been joined mentally, they had never touched each other in a sexual way; but somehow, it seemed right now that Kendall was there. Tentatively, he swiped Sutter's tongue with his. Concentrating, Sutter delved into the bond and felt the same strong need in Josh that he had felt in himself at the first accidental contact. Suddenly, they were exploring each other's mouths, shocked by the unexpected pleasure it brought.

Kendall shivered as their enjoyment rippled through the mental interface. She opened her eyes. How erotic it was to watch her lovers kiss! Her pussy throbbed and she crossed her legs, bringing them together tightly, arching as her climax washed over her.

Josh immersed himself in the flood of sensation roaring into him from Kendall. It was so good to be able to feel what she felt, to know what it was like for a woman — to feel what having her breasts sucked did for her. To ride her orgasm. To know that seeing him and Sutter touching one another turned her on. He savored the knowledge of just how wildly horny the two of them could make her.

As Kendall relaxed and the orgasm faded, they withdrew. Josh returned to the stove and whipped up some scrambled eggs, while Sutter and Kendall sat at the table and sipped orange juice. Occasionally, Sutter would reach out and run his cool glass over the tip of one of Kendall's nipples, and she would shudder, meeting his eyes boldly. Josh brought the eggs over to the table and dished them out onto plates. Kendall sprinkled salt on her breakfast and set the salt shaker aside.

"Ooops." Josh bent over and closed his mouth on Kendall's right breast, drawing the nipple slowly up and out as he sucked briefly, then released it. "You had some salt right — there," he said, touching his fingertip to the apex of her bud, buzzing with renewed desire. Kendall took a shaky breath and made another attempt to eat.

"Could you pass me the salt, Sutter?" Sutter picked up the salt shaker and passed it across the table to Josh, deliberately brushing across Kendall's nipples with the backs of his knuckles as he did so. Kendall moaned and dropped her fork, burying her face in her hands. "I don't think I can take this."

Sutter grinned mischievously. "Too hot for you? Here, maybe this will help." He removed a piece of ice from his glass and began rubbing one edge over her tingling breast. Kendall moaned again and arched her back. Josh took her other nipple in his warm mouth. The contrast was intoxicating. Then they switched, Sutter's mouth closing on her stiff cold bud, and it was all Kendall could do to keep from crying out. She grasped the nearest hand — Josh's — and pushed it toward her crotch. He and Sutter both pulled away. "We'd better finish eating before everything gets cold," they said.

Kendall groaned. They were purposefully making her wait. While it was maddening, it was also very sexy. With each passing moment, the crotch of her shorts became more damp and her nipples were swollen to the point of aching. She cleaned her plate as quickly as she could and waited expectantly. Sutter looked at her with a twinkle in his eyes and a bland expression. "Why don't you go wait in the living room while we clean up?"

"Aargh!" Kendall exclaimed, frustrated, but she pushed back her chair and left the room. She flopped onto the couch, restless and primed. After a moment, she cocked one leg and feathered her fingers lightly along her inner thigh. No reason she couldn't touch herself. Just for a minute. Just to make the wait a little easier. Idly, she dipped two fingers into her wet cunt.

"That's a no-no." Sutter came up behind her, grabbed her elbow and pulled her hand from her crotch. He leaned over the couch and brought her fingers up to his nose, inhaling her scent. "Your pussy belongs to us today. Unless we tell you otherwise." He buried the offending digits in his mouth and sucked her juices from them noisily. He let go and came around, then pulled her up from the couch, covering her mouth in his. Kendall could taste her essence on his lips. Once again, the taste of herself on another person's tongue birthed a powerful tide of lust within her.

Sutter sat down and patted the cushion next to him. Kendall sat just as Josh came in from the kitchen. He joined them on the couch. Nodding to Josh, Sutter slipped his hand inside her pants leg. "Mmmm." Kendall brought her legs up, resting her heels on the edge of the cushion. "Here you go, baby," Sutter whispered, sliding his thumb inside her pussy, oriented upwards, massaging as he slowly glided it in and out. Josh's thumb joined his, facing the opposite direction, kneading the back wall of her vagina. "Oh, yes," Kendall whispered. "Yes." She began pumping her hips back and forth.

"That's it, baby," Sutter murmured. "Mmmm. I love the feel of your hot, wet pussy."

"Faster, baby," Josh urged. "Come for us."

Kendall moaned, driving her hips faster and faster.

"That's it, baby," they said in unison, rubbing harder. Deeper. Kendall's pussy convulsed briefly. "Oh, yeah," they breathed. "That's it. Squeeze, baby. Squeeze." Kendall gasped, contracting her pussy determinedly.

"God, yes!" Sutter moaned. He reached inside his shorts.

Kendall clamped her knees together, trapping their thumbs inside her as she held her breath while the climax ripped through her. "Yes!" Sutter roared, pumping his cock as semen spurted from its tip.

Kendall turned her head. She could feel Josh's mind, feel how he was holding back. Always holding back. She caressed his cheek. "Why do you do that?" she whispered. "Come for me, Josh." She pushed the waistband of his shorts down so that she could see his magnificent cock.

"Please, Josh. I want to see you come." She took his hand in hers and wrapped it around his swollen member. "Come for me, Josh." She urged his hand up and down. She spread her thighs and pulled Sutter's hand from between her legs, guiding it to Josh's manhood. Josh moaned. "That's it," she whispered. Together, the three of them caressed Josh's staff.

Sutter liked the feel of Josh's rod in his hand. He could feel Josh's control weakening. Abruptly, he wrapped his hand firmly around the lower half of Josh's cock. He sent Josh and Kendall mental images of what he wanted them to do. Josh's hand closed tight on the upper half of his penis. Kendall captured the flushed head between the tips of her fingers, rotating them round and round its thick circumference. Slowly, then faster and faster, Josh and Sutter milked his cock together while Kendall played with his head until he thought he would explode. The dam collapsed, and Josh's cock did exactly that. Kendall smiled as pearly iridescence spangled his abdomen.

Josh ran shaking hands through his dark hair. "Damn!" he said. He rested for a minute. "Damn," he said again, apparently at a loss for other words. Sutter and Kendall basked in the warm flood of satisfaction that emanated from him.

"You have to stop doing that," Kendall admonished.

"What?" Josh asked.

"Holding back."

Josh blushed.

"Why do you do that?"

Josh shook his head. "I don't know. I'm just like that. Even in the bond, it's hard for me to open up completely. I'm kind of like you, I guess. Trying to keep from being hurt because of things that have happened in the past. Only I haven't dealt with it as well as you have."

"Who hurt you, Josh?"

He looked away. Kendall slipped to the floor and leaned forward, running her tongue along the top of his thigh, cleaning his seed from him. "Hmmm?" she murmured. "Who?"

He shook his head, looking down at her. "Are you trying to bribe me?"

Kendall grinned. "Is it working?" She tickled the tip of his cock with her tongue.

Josh groaned, but began talking as he watched her. "My mom died in a car accident when I was two. My dad — well, he never got over it, I guess." Josh's tone was bitter, and Kendall raised her eyebrows questioningly. "He was a drunk. We lived on welfare and money he got from odd jobs and selling off things that used to be my mother's. I was only able to go to Whitecliff — that's the private school where Sutter and I met — because I had this great teacher in second grade. I'm kind of a whiz at science and math, and she saw my potential and went out and found someone to sponsor me at Whitecliff, so I started there in third grade."

"That's great," Kendall said softly.

"Yeah. I didn't realize how much she'd done for me until I was older, of course. But eventually I did. I tried to find out who my sponsor was once, to thank them; but the security on records of confidential donations to Whitecliff is incredible. I can hack into financial institutions, but I can't break into Whitecliff's donor database."

Kendall raised her eyebrows. "Hacking?"

Josh reddened again.

"It's stupid." He shook his head. "I'm—kind of a genius with computers, too. I hacked into Sutter's dad's bank when I was fifteen. I transferred a bunch of money from his accounts into a dummy account that I created." Kendall was staring at him with wide eyes. "We didn't touch the money," he insisted. "It was basically a way of getting even with him for trying to keep us apart."

"See," Sutter interjected, "When we started high school, my dad kind of went berserk over how close we were. He thought we were gay. I tried to explain to him how it was, but he didn't believe me. We just wanted him to sweat a little." He nodded as Kendall frowned. "I know. Stupid. But we were just kids. Anyway, they found it and traced it back to Josh before we could put the money back."

"Luckily," Josh finished, "I was considered such a good boy—great recommendations from my teachers, excellent grades, all that jazz—that since we hadn't spent the money and I'd never been in trouble before, I just got probation."

Kendall licked the last drop of semen from his belly and sat up, leaning back against the coffee table. She looked at Sutter. "That must have made things with your dad even more difficult."

Sutter grimaced. "He was furious, sure. But it was kind of weird. After he found out what we did, he sat me down and told me I could resume the friendship, as long as I could promise him we hadn't ever touched each other in a sexual way.

"I mean, I had already told him we weren't gay, but this time he seemed to believe me, and he left us alone after that." Josh tensed and Sutter frowned. "Until now, anyway."

Kendall looked from one to the other, sensing a sudden strong tension through the bond. "Did something happen?" Kendall asked.

"He's on a campaign to get rid of me," Josh said bitterly.

Sutter nodded. "Basically, he's threatening to cut me off if I don't quit playing around and get serious. To quote him, I've got to 'stop fucking up in school and start acting normal, find a girl, get married.' Get rid of Josh."

"What do you mean—cut you off?"

"My dad pays the mortgage on this place. The utilities. Hell, he pays for everything, including groceries and the car."

"Why?" Kendall said. "I mean, I can understand him supporting you while you go to college, but if he dislikes Josh so much why would he pay for all this, knowing that he's living here?" She swept her arm out, indicating the house.

"Because he'd rather pay for us to build a house out in the boondocks where we live together, than have his friends knowing that we're living in town together."

"Lots of people in college have roommates, Sutter. I don't think—"

"We're different, though. We don't hide how close we are. We can't. And Dad knows that. People talk about us. At first they think we're gay. Eventually, they figure we're not. But they still sense there's something different about us, and it bothers them. And that bothers my dad. He can't handle it. He's third generation Texas lawyer. Powerful, tough macho man. Appearances are important to him."

"What about school? *Are* you having trouble?"

"Only because his heart's not in it," Josh said before Sutter could answer.

"What do you mean?"

"Sutter doesn't want to be a lawyer. He *hates* law."

"Do you?" she asked Sutter. He sighed and rested his head back on the couch, staring at the ceiling. Sadness, anger and regret were swirling through the bond.

"Yes."

"What do you really want to do?" Kendall prompted. Sutter shook his head and didn't answer.

"Tell her, Sutter." Josh reached over and nudged him in the ribs, but Sutter ignored him. Josh sighed. "He wants to be an artist."

"I remember. You said something about that last night."

Josh nodded. "He only thinks he's no good at it because that's what his dad's been telling him all his life. David Campbell wants Sutter to be just like him. Go to law school, marry some society babe that knows how to play the game. Have another boy to carry on the Campbell tradition. Art's not an acceptable alternative." He grimaced. "Nothing would be. David's got Sutter's life mapped out for him, and I'm an unexpected detour. He wants me erased." He pointed toward the staircase. "Look at those carvings." There was fierce pride in his voice. "I mean, just look at them. Have you ever seen anything like it? One reason David doesn't like me is because I keep encouraging Sutter to do what he really loves."

Kendall had been too preoccupied the night before, and even that morning, to notice the posts supporting the banister up to the second floor. She stood and walked over to the stairs. The posts had been hand carved and sanded satin-smooth—each one a sleek, slender representation of a different ocean denizen, both real and fantastic. There was a dolphin, a mermaid, a narwhal, a sea horse; and as Josh had said, Kendall had never seen anything like them. She recalled the carvings above the front door and windows that she had seen the night before and remembered that he had done those as well. "These are unbelievable, Sutter," she breathed. She turned and stared at him. "Why haven't you—"

"My dad may be a jerk," Sutter interrupted, "But outside of Josh, and now you, he's all I have. My mom was a Scandinavian model. She moved back there after they got divorced, and we hardly ever talk. I've had about a half dozen stepmothers, and I didn't like a single one, and they didn't like me. I don't think it's that wrong for him to want me to follow in his footsteps."

"It is if following in his footsteps makes you miserable." Kendall walked back into the living room and sat down on the coffee table. "What does *your* dad think of your relationship with Sutter, Josh?"

"Actually, my dad's the one person who never thought we were anything more than friends. He was usually too drunk to pay any attention to us. He used to tell me 'Josh, you're doin' the right thing, hangin' round that Campbell kid. He's gonna be big some day. Can't hurt to ride on his coat tails, now, can it?' Just before he passed out." Josh was quiet for a long moment, then continued. "That's why we always hung out at my house, because all my dad did was watch TV and drink all day long. He pretty much didn't care what we were doing as long as we made his beer runs and kept him fed."

"And now that you're out of the house? Do you keep in touch?"

Josh stared unseeingly at a spot just above Kendall's head. "He's dead," he answered woodenly. "Died last year. Liver failure."

Kendall's sorrow mingled with theirs through the bond. They were right. The longer she spent with them, the easier it became for her to tap into the connection; to read their thoughts and feelings without the necessity of touch. "I'm sorry," she whispered. Josh shrugged as if it didn't matter, but he swallowed thickly. He wouldn't meet her eyes. "Are you happy with what you're doing?" she asked. "Studying to become an architect? Living here on David Campbell's good graces?" she finished.

A red flush crept over Josh's cheeks. "I don't have any family, Kendall. Or any money. I'm going to college on scholarships. Yeah, I could start working and live in some student apartment in town, take fewer classes, but…"

"I'm not trying to shame you, Josh," Kendall interrupted softly. "I'm asking if you're happy." Once again, Kendall considered the difference in their ages. The gap between twenty-two and thirty-two suddenly seemed terribly pronounced. "Do you really want to be an architect?"

"Yes."

"Okay, so you're happy with your career choice." She turned to Sutter. "What about you? What do you really want to do with your life?"

Sutter raised his head. The usual look of utter confidence had disappeared. Instead, he looked older, tired. But he didn't answer. "Sutter. I want to help. Tell me what you want." Sutter had been so demanding, even controlling, in the few days she'd known him. She expected to see that defense mechanism yet again but suddenly, he was like a lost little boy. She opened her heart to him, allowing the love that she was feeling to flow into him, willing him to open up to her. He closed his eyes. "I hate living off my dad," he admitted. "I hate Law," he added vehemently. "It would be nice to just—be me," he said.

"Thank you." Kendall thought for a moment, then continued briskly. "Here's what we do. Is this house in your name or your father's?"

Sutter looked puzzled. "Actually, it's in mine and Josh's name. I told my dad that's the only way I'd do it. If something happened to me, I didn't want him to be able to take the house from Josh."

"That's good. So, what about us? Were you serious about wanting this to be a long-term, permanent relationship?"

The two of them stared, offended. "How can you ask?" Sutter protested, "Can't you feel it?"

Kendall nodded. "I can. But I wanted to be sure." She looked down at the floor, her brusque confidence suddenly overshadowed by a troubled uncertainty. "Because here's the deal. I'm thirty-two years old. If there's one thing I've learned, it's that you need to deal with problems right up front. This relationship is going to be pretty damn interesting even without any additional pressures. I want us to have the best chance possible to make it. And that means we have to be completely honest, not just with each other, but in how we live our lives."

Kendall could feel Josh weighing her words, calculating. "What does that mean?"

Kendall looked up. "It means—" she hesitated, then met Sutter's gaze squarely. "I can fix this. I can move out here," she held up a quelling hand at Sutter's slow grin. Josh was watching shrewdly. She could feel that he knew what was coming. "The girl who works for me has been looking for her own apartment, and she loves mine. I'll rent it to her. I can move out here and make the house payment, the utilities. Even the car. I can support us until Josh graduates from college and gets a job.

"But you have to quit, Sutter." His gaze narrowed, and she swallowed nervously before continuing. "You have to give yourself a chance at what it is you really want. You have to try to establish yourself as an artist."

He started to protest, but she reached out and grabbed his knee, talking urgently. "I can help. I've done it."

Sutter shook his head. "Please." Kendall looked at him, her eyes bright and determined. "I love you, but I won't do this. If I come into this relationship the way things are now, it won't work."

"Kendall—"

"It's true," she insisted. With sudden insight, she looked at Josh. "It's one of the reasons Josh holds back."

Sutter chuckled, looking to his friend for support, but Josh nodded. "Why?" Sutter asked.

"Because I know you're not happy, and it eats at me. Plus, you give in to your dad more and more as time passes. Ultimately—I guess I'm afraid that one day David's going to manage to finally drive that wedge between us."

Chapter Seven
Parlor Games

"Let's start out on the right track, Sutter." Kendall's heart was pounding, worried what he might decide. She was absolutely serious. She wasn't going to come into this knowing already that one of them was unhappy. Too much potential for failure and turmoil. Not that there wouldn't be strain anyway, if Sutter decided to finally stand up to his father. But at least it would be open, honest tension, for all the right reasons. Not something beneath the surface that ate away at them and undermined their relationship.

Sutter finally smiled. "You're going to change everything, aren't you?"

"Hopefully for the better."

Sutter leaned forward. "Deal," he whispered just before he claimed her mouth. He unsnapped her shorts and tugged down her zipper. Kendall stood, Sutter moving with her, exploring her mouth with his tongue as she slid her shorts down and tossed them aside.

Sutter guided her to a sitting position on the rug, his hands slipping under her blouse. Kendall raised her arms and Sutter pulled the blouse off, letting it drop. Kendall shivered as Josh came up behind her and began kissing his way down her back. Kendall pushed Sutter's shorts down, releasing his cock, and he lay back against the floor.

Kendall straddled him. His cock tested the opening to her vagina, but she was swollen and tight after all the unaccustomed activity of the night before. Kendall supported herself on her knees while she reached between her thighs and pulled her tender labia apart. She lowered herself onto him, her pussy enveloping him like a custom-made glove. Sutter grasped her waist, helping her to move up and down, deliciously slow and deliberate.

Kendall leaned forward, letting the peaks of her tingling nipples brush lightly across his chest with the rhythm of their movements. Josh knelt behind her and a moment later she felt his fingers pulling her butt cheeks apart, and a corkscrew of delight warmed her pussy as she anticipated what he might do.

But what happened next was almost more than she could bear. Warm, searching wetness. Josh's tongue, lapping at her anus. Kendall gasped, her pussy convulsing involuntarily, erratically, on Sutter's long cock. "Mmmm," Sutter murmured. Kendall breathed heavily as Josh's tongue disappeared. She felt him massaging her anus with two of his fingers, then gently inserting the tip of first one, then the other, just past the rim. Separating them slightly, he held the tiny portal open. Kendall moaned as her cunt spasmed again. "Yes, Kendall," Sutter murmured. "Come for us." In the next instant, Josh was tasting her with his tongue again, burying the tip inside her this time. "Oh God," Kendall groaned. "Josh." The tip of his tongue wiggled. "Yes, Josh!" She screamed his name repeatedly as her every muscle and organ seemed to flame with hot desire at once. Her sudden excitement rippled through the bond and Sutter gasped, unable to delay his climax. His semen poured into a body so consumed by heat and passion that his essence flowing into her was like a cool stream of water poured into the gaping mouth of a volcano, barely quenching her desire. Kendall, still trapped in the throes of passion, gasped in frustration as he deflated.

Sensing her need, Josh sat up and Sutter quickly lifted her from him, turning her onto her back. Kendall breathed hard, clutching Josh's shoulders as he positioned himself above her and buried his thick cock inside her, pouring his own essence onto the flame burning within her as she continued to writhe, convulsing on his cock over and over.

Finally, the contractions began to fade and the conflagration was extinguished. Kendall lay breathless on the floor, drenched in sweat. Josh and Sutter lay on their sides next to her, smoothing damp curls back from her face, watching her with satisfaction and a possessiveness that thrilled her to the bone.

"How can you make me come like that?" she whispered.

"We're soul mates," Josh murmured.

Kendall sighed contentedly. They lay together on the floor for a while, dozing, until Kendall sat up and pulled on her clothes. "I'm hungry," she announced. Josh and Sutter dressed quickly, then followed her into the kitchen, where the three of them fixed sandwiches. Sitting at the table, they chatted amiably as they ate.

"When do you think you'll be moving in?" Josh asked eventually.

Kendall shrugged. "Let me talk to Brandy. Find out when she can take over the apartment." She glanced at Sutter. "Are you okay with all of this?"

"Yeah." He made a face. "Josh is right. It's time I stood up to my dad. If I let things go on the way they are, either my dad's going to win or I'll just be doing this later. And it would be even harder to do later." Kendall searched his eyes, and he reached out and squeezed her shoulder, smiling. "I'm fine. Really. I *need* someone who will kick me in the butt every now and then." He caressed her shoulder with his thumb. "It's hard to stand up for what you want when you don't feel like you have it yet. This will be a lot easier for me, now that we're complete."

After they had finished eating, Kendall helped Josh rinse the dishes and put them in the dishwasher. Sutter wandered into the den and picked up a pool cue. "Do you play?" he asked.

"I love pool," Kendall confessed. "But I'm not all that good at it."

"That's okay." Sutter racked up the balls and grabbed a cue while Josh flopped onto the recliner to watch.

Kendall broke, and called stripes. But Sutter was definitely a good player, and it wasn't long before Kendall had been defeated. Josh took Sutter's place. Kendall and Josh were more evenly matched, and the game lasted quite a while, until only one each of their balls and the eight-ball remained. Kendall bent over the table, her shorts tight across her butt, and Sutter's fingers itched to reach out and touch her. Josh, meanwhile, was mesmerized by the glimpse he was getting of her generous cleavage. Kendall lined up and made her shot.

"Scratch," Sutter said, standing up with a mischievous gleam in his eyes. "You know what *that* means."

Josh raised his eyebrows quizzically. Kendall turned to stare at Sutter, curiosity and anticipation tickling her tummy. Sutter reached out, wordlessly removing her shirt. Then he unsnapped her shorts and removed them as well.

Kendall laughed breathlessly. "Why don't I just leave these off for the rest of the day, so we don't have to keep taking them off?"

Sutter's eyes blazed. "Perfect."

Kendall swallowed past a nervous lump of excitement as Sutter advanced. He picked her up and placed her on one end of the pool table. "Turn around," he said, and she obliged, bringing her legs up and onto the table. "Now, spread your legs," he murmured into her ear. Kendall brought her knees up and parted her legs, grasping the edge of the table behind her and leaning back. Josh grinned and grabbed his cue.

"Two-ball," he said, "Right — there." He touched Kendall's glistening pussy with the tip of his stick. Kendall watched in fascination as he made the shot, his ball rolling up and nestling gently in the moist hollow between her legs.

Grinning, Sutter parted the lips of her vagina and rolled the ball back and forth, round and round against the wet flesh, coating the sphere with Kendall's juices. He held it up to her mouth. "Lick it," he whispered. Kendall stuck out her tongue and ran it across the smooth, sticky surface. "Mmmm," Sutter murmured. "I like that." He turned the ball as Kendall continued to clean her essence from it, enjoying the two rapt gazes concentrating on her mouth.

"Damn," Sutter mumbled as she sucked the last of her juices from the ball. He grabbed a couple more balls, as did Josh, and began rolling them over her body, kneading her flesh. Kendall scooted to the middle of the table, lying back and closing her eyes as she enjoyed this most erotic massage. One of them pushed her legs apart and began rolling a couple of balls over and around her throbbing clit, burying one between the lips of her vagina. "Mmmmm, yes," Kendall murmured.

Inspired, Sutter separated the two halves of his cue stick. Shaking with anticipation, he glanced at Kendall to make sure her eyes were still closed and went into the living room. Returning with a bottle of lotion, he squirted some into his hands and coated the handle of his cue with the slippery solution. Josh realized his intention and waited until he was ready, then removed the balls he was tormenting Kendall's crotch with and watched raptly as Sutter plunged the handle of his cue stick into Kendall's dripping cunt.

Kendall gasped as something cold and hard buried itself in her pussy. Startled, she opened her eyes and pushed herself up slightly. Sutter's gaze was challenging. Her eyes traveled to the implement he had buried inside her, and she licked her lips. Reaching out, she covered his hand with her own. Sutter grinned as Kendall's insistent fingers pushed against his, urging him to drive the cue even deeper. He complied, watching her face as her gaze locked onto her crotch. Kendall let go of his hand, pushing herself up a little more, breathing rapidly as he bore it deeper, thrusting her hips forward. "Fuck it for me, baby," he urged.

Kendall took the stick slowly, at first. As Sutter withdrew it, she moaned, stimulated by the sight of her opalescent juices coating the dark wood. Sutter watched her pussy, fascinated. Her large lips dipped in as she thrust up, then slid out, hugging the implement as though reluctant to let go. "God, Kendall," he groaned, sending her a quick image of what he was seeing. She gasped, moving faster as Sutter guided it deeper and deeper. She pictured Sutter playing pool tomorrow, a year from now, handling something that had been buried inside her. At the thought, her limited restraint snapped and she grasped the cue with both hands. Sutter let go and Josh reached out to support her hips, holding them still while she plunged the rod in as far as it would go. They both watched as she bucked frantically, fucking herself. Sutter reached out and stimulated her clit with one finger, and that was all it took for Kendall to arch, her mouth open in a wordless scream as a rush of intense gratification pulsed through her core.

Sutter and Josh both groaned. Their cocks strained against their shorts. "I love watching you fuck yourself," Josh whispered in Kendall's ear. She opened her eyes and met Josh's gaze as she slipped Sutter's cue from her crotch. "Where's yours?" she asked in a voice husky with desire.

Josh let go of her hips and grabbed his cue stick eagerly, separating the two halves while she watched. He squirted lotion onto the handle and moved toward the table as Sutter took up position behind Kendall, supporting her hips as Josh had done. Josh inched his stick into her cunt slowly, ignoring her eager urgings, pleased to know that making her wait drove her wild. Once again, Kendall watched avidly as her lover's pool cue disappeared inside her, becoming desperate and pleading as Josh continued to move the rod slowly and deliberately, drawing back when she bucked, resisting her efforts to force it deeper. "Please, Josh," she finally begged, her entire body trembling. "Please. I need it." Josh smiled and nodded to Sutter, then imbedded the stick in her pussy as Sutter immobilized her hips. "Yes!" To her eyes, the stick became a blur as Josh pumped it in and out more and more rapidly, the muscles in his arm rippling; until finally, Kendall froze, her pussy convulsing repeatedly against the now-warm wood. Josh licked his lips as her contractions forced her thick juices to ooze out past the circumference of the pool cue. He couldn't resist. He bent over and licked the tantalizing seepage from her labia. "Mmmmm," Kendall moaned, wiggling slightly. Encouraged, Josh removed the pool stick and splayed her legs. Beckoning to Sutter, he bent over her crotch again. Sutter lay Kendall gently back on the table.

Kendall closed her eyes as Josh buried his tongue in her vagina and Sutter's lips kissed her clit. "Oh, yes," she murmured. "I like that." Standing to either side of the pool table, Josh and Sutter turned their heads to face each other, then dipped their tongues in and out of Kendall's pussy, sometimes alternating, sometimes at the same time, sometimes even allowing their tongues to dance together briefly as they had earlier in the kitchen. Being with Kendall heightened their sexuality in ways they hadn't expected. Sutter found himself wondering what it would be like to be touched by Josh.

Josh felt a thrill go through him as he sensed Sutter's musing. He met Sutter's eye. "Later?" he asked. Swallowing hard, Sutter nodded and Josh smiled. Then Sutter drew back.

Kendall moaned as Sutter's lips withdrew. Sutter reached out and pushed Kendall's closest knee back toward her chest. He took her hand and placed it behind her knee. He walked around and did the same at her other side, guiding her supporting hands out to the side, so that her gleaming pussy was open wide, and her generous derriere was easily accessible. With one glance, Josh understood what he intended, and bent to the task. Kendall squirmed restlessly, her eyes still closed, holding her legs for her lovers, willing them to resume pleasuring her cunt with their tongues. She jerked involuntarily as

Sutter began teasing her clit again. A moment later, she felt Josh pulling on her right buttock as Sutter did the same with the left. Gasping, she arched her back as Josh's warm tongue massaged the opening of her anus insistently. "Oh God, yes," Kendall murmured, surprising herself by puckering her anus, then relaxing it, trying to entice his tongue into the tight opening.

Sutter licked his way down to her vagina, watching Josh's ministrations as he went. He wondered again at how incredibly erotic it was to watch the two people he loved touching one another.

Kendall sensed his thought, and wished she could see, as well. He was right. And it was also incredibly stimulating to watch herself touch them, or to watch them touch her. Then she couldn't think anymore, because Sutter was drinking from her pussy while Josh's tongue pushed into her anus — probing, exploring, giving rise to indescribably magnificent sensations in Kendall's groin.

"Oh, God," Kendall moaned. She wanted to let go of her legs and grasp the edges of the table, but she was afraid they wouldn't be able to continue pleasuring both portals. Breathing hard, she arched back her head, desperately contracting and releasing the muscles of both her pussy and her anus, silently urging them deeper.

Their grips tightened on her buttocks, pulling them even farther apart, though that didn't seem possible, allowing Josh to penetrate her ass almost fully with his tongue. Kendall surprised herself again — unable to speak, she found herself grunting and whimpering, begging them in a primal language to make her come.

Sutter buried his tongue in her cunt, breathing deeply, drawing her scent into his lungs. Playfully, he nipped at her vaginal walls with his teeth. "God, yes!" Kendall urged between gasps. "Yes." A flood of sensations washed over her from her lovers. Kendall dove into the silent communication. Sutter was thinking how hungry he was—how no matter how much of her pussy he ate, it would never be enough. Josh's tongue was now plunging in and out of her anus, but in his mind, he was picturing himself watching his cock do the same. "God, yes Josh!" Kendall rasped, forming a similar picture in her mind, willing him to make it come true.

The sudden intensity of Kendall's desire—the image she had conjured, superimposed on his—ripped through Josh's abdomen. His semen jetted from his cock with such rapid force it was almost painful and he stood up suddenly and grabbed the edge of the table for support, biting his lip to keep from crying out.

The three of them were so synchronized, Sutter roared and Kendall screamed as her pussy and Sutter's cock pulsed in rhythm with Josh's release. Kendall's grip slipped, and she let her legs hang off either side of the pool table as she collapsed against the green expanse.

Wordlessly, steeling his weak legs, Josh gathered Kendall into his arms. Muscles bulging, Sutter leading the way, he carried Kendall up the stairs and into the bedroom, depositing her carefully on the bed. Kendall smiled and stretched luxuriously as they stood looking down at her. Sutter moved to the dresser and took something from one of the drawers, then came and sat on the bed beside her. He grasped one of her wrists and lifted it to the headboard, fixing it in place with one of the two ties he had taken from the drawer. A slight twinge of apprehension caused Kendall to shiver; but she was absolutely convinced neither Sutter nor Josh would ever hurt her, so she offered her other wrist voluntarily, winning a dazzling grin from Sutter and a gaze that sparked with unbridled passion from Josh.

Josh rummaged in the dresser while Sutter finished tying Kendall's wrist, then came over and sat at the foot of the bed. "We bought some toys yesterday, while we were waiting to pick you up." He spread his bounty on the cover. Kendall looked down, trying to see over her tummy, but the items were hidden from view. She tried to sit up, but with her wrists fastened to the headboard, she was unable to rise up enough to see. Josh smiled knowingly. He squatted at the foot of the bed, turning something she couldn't see over and over in his hands as he met her gaze. "You've had a particular thought," he said.

Kendall swallowed. "Which one?" she whispered hoarsely.

Josh grinned mischievously and slipped his finger between her butt cheeks, toying with the mouth of her anus. "Did you like it with our tongues?" Kendall nodded desperately. "Do you really want us to do that with our cocks?" he asked. Licking her lips in anticipation, Kendall nodded once again. "Then we have some work to do." He held up the object in his hand. It was a slender dildo, not much wider than a finger, nor much longer. "We'll have to make some preparations." Sutter handed him a bottle of lubricant, and Kendall watched as Josh covered the small white rod with the glimmering substance. Sutter sat by her side on the bed, playing idly with one of her nipples as he watched Josh. When Josh was ready, Sutter reached out and pulled Kendall's legs back against her stomach, lifting her butt into the air. Josh's breathing quickened as he squirted a stream of lubricant into her crack, then rubbed it over her buttocks and around the opening of her anus.

Kendall gasped with pleasure as he slipped the tip of his forefinger into the tight little pucker. He massaged the rim of her anus with his fingertip, penetrating her slightly as well, so as to rub some of the lubricant inside the canal. Capturing her gaze with his, he replaced his finger with the hard, smooth dildo.

Kendall met his gaze unflinchingly, her green eyes dark with desire as the cool tool slid inexorably inside her. "Oh, yes," she murmured. Sutter began titillating her clit with the tip of one nail. "Yes," Kendall moaned. Josh stopped with the toy only halfway inside her, watching her eyes.

"Do you like it?" he whispered.

"Yes," Kendall murmured.

"What do you want me to do?" he prompted.

"Deeper," Kendall gasped. He pushed it in a little farther, then stopped again. Kendall whimpered. Sutter's fingertip was driving her crazy, and Josh's slow progress was sheer torment. "Deeper," she pleaded. Josh inched the tool in farther. "Mmmm. Yes." Grinning, Josh eased the dildo in until it had penetrated as fully as possible. He pumped it in and out a few times experimentally, fascinated as Kendall's passion and need washed through him, her eyes becoming unfocused as she bit her lip and wished he would go faster.

Instead, he removed the dildo. "No," Kendall groaned. He picked up another toy and showed it to her. Kendall's breath came rapidly as she studied the new object. About as wide as two fingers, its rubbery, flesh-colored surface was covered with small ridges. Kendall waited fervently as Josh applied lubricant, then smeared a little more into her crack. Josh forced the tips of two of his fingers into the pink, swollen pucker. Kendall gasped and bit her lip. Josh looked at her with concern.

"Do you want me to stop?" Kendall shook her head. Josh penetrated a little farther, experimentally, and when Kendall arched her back and thrust her hips toward him, he began massaging the interior of her tight canal, captivated by the quiet sounds of pleasure and frustration she made. Finally, he pulled out his fingers and, holding her cheeks wide, began to force the new toy into her anus. Kendall gasped loudly. Sutter took one of her hands in his. Kendall squeezed as Josh slowly, carefully infiltrated her ass with the textured dildo. At its widest point, she winced involuntarily.

"Does it hurt?" Sutter asked. Kendall nodded, her eyes closed tight. "Should we stop?" Shaking her head, Kendall concentrated on how it felt, allowing her sensations to flow into her two lovers.

Sutter closed his eyes as pure lust washed over him. Yes, Kendall was feeling some pain, but it only served to heighten her sensitivity to the vast pleasure she was also feeling. He sensed her gut clenching in desire, her nipples tingling, her anus throbbing—and her hungry pussy, desperate for something to milk. Letting go of her hand, he reached out and pick up a third dildo, thicker and longer than the other two.

Kendall arched and cried out as something thick and hard plumbed her pussy. She opened her eyes and glanced down, watching as Sutter plunged this third toy deep inside her cunt. "Please, please," Kendall moaned.

"Please what?" Sutter asked, continuing his vigorous fucking.

Kendall moaned wordlessly, tossing her head back and forth. Deep, hard, and fast, they plunged their tools into her over and over. Kendall felt them colliding against each other, inside her, trapping sensitive tissue between them in moments of exquisite torture.

Josh and Sutter buried themselves in her sensations, reveling in the satisfaction she was feeling at having both holes fucked at once—again catching that desperate wish to have both their cocks inside her simultaneously. Josh and Sutter looked at each other. Josh quickly removed the knobby dildo from her ass and reached for the final toy—one that was as long and thick as Sutter's cock. Kendall was bucking frantically, Sutter not even having to move his hand as she fucked the toy he held. Josh squirted liberal amounts of lubricant onto this largest dildo, then parted Kendall's ass again. As much as he wanted to, he couldn't do this slowly. The convergent needs of three people pushed him to the limit, and he couldn't maintain his methodical self-control. He grabbed the bottle of lubricant and placed the tip just inside Kendall's anus, squeezing fluid into her canal until it seeped out around the tip.

"Yes, yes!" Kendall relaxed her lower body as best she could, in anticipation of another delicious penetration. She wasn't disappointed. Groaning, Josh shoved the substitute cock far up inside her.

Kendall bit her lip to keep from crying out, afraid any such sound would make Josh stop. The stinging undercurrent of pain was nothing compared to the shudders of pleasure hammering her body. Rapidly, frantically, Josh and Sutter both fucked her with their toys.

Kendall tossed her head from side to side. "God, Josh. Please," she moaned.

"What is it, baby?" he murmured.

"I want the real thing," she rasped. "Please. Both of you."

Kendall's ardent need was a wild blaze humming through the two of them. Josh plumbed Kendall's anus a couple more times. The tight canal offered strong resistance, but Josh watched Kendall's face carefully; there was no hint of discomfort on her features or in her thoughts, only agitated urgency and concentrated pleasure.

Josh pulled out the dildo and tossed it aside. He couldn't believe he was hard again, but the thought of having anal sex with Kendall had been enough to make it so. Sutter withdrew the other dildo, and Kendall lay panting as he reached up and untied her wrists from the bedposts. He held out his hand, and guided Kendall off the bed. She stood on limbs watery with anticipation. Sutter and Josh hesitated, eying one another. After a moment, during which they appeared to reach a silent agreement, Josh lay across the bed. His cock was much thicker than Sutter's, and although he was aching to take her that way, this was the first time and he didn't want to hurt her. With his feet on the floor, he positioned his crotch right at the edge of the bed. He beckoned to Kendall.

Kendall mounted him, sighing with satisfaction as his fat rod packed her pussy. Josh reached for her shoulders and pulled her face to his, tangling his hands in her hair, stoking the inferno in her groin with his kiss.

Sutter grabbed a short padded bench from under the bed and placed it on the floor between Josh's feet. He knelt on the bench, which placed his cock at exactly the right level.

Kendall felt Sutter's hands pushing her legs forward. Kendall pulled her knees up onto the bed, as far and as close to Josh's body as she could. A moment later, she felt Sutter's muscular hands rubbing the lubricant between her cheeks. Kendall sighed and wiggled slightly. Her inflamed pussy was demanding desperately that she ride Josh's cock, but she knew she needed to wait. Sutter's slippery finger entered her anus, and Kendall's breathing quickened, a flush suffusing her cheeks. As Josh had done, he inserted the tip of the bottle and squirted lubricant inside, and Kendall gasped. Josh captured her face in his hands, holding her gaze with his, wanting to see the look on her face when Sutter penetrated her. She felt Sutter's hands parting her ass and held her breath in expectation. Again, Sutter's finger slipped inside her, exploring, stimulating. Kendall began to moan, her eyes glazing over. "That's it, baby," Josh whispered. "That's it." Kendall's breath caught as Sutter slipped in a second finger, parting them slightly within her, twisting them like a corkscrew, loosening that tight opening. "Yes." Kendall prompted. Sutter shivered and spread his fingers farther apart.

Sutter's warm, wet tongue invaded her. She sobbed with need. "Sutter, please. I want your cock. Please." Josh watched her intently, his limbs melting with the strength of the sensations flooding into him from his two lovers — the savage spears of craving that pierced Kendall's core as Sutter tasted her; Sutter's urge to dominate Kendall, to make her beg for more. Josh arched his back and moaned as his own body responded with a surge of feral lust that set his teeth on edge. Suddenly, he wanted *everything*. He wanted to fuck *both* his partners. Kendall *and* Sutter. He imagined himself buried in Kendall's cunt while he drank from Sutter's long, hard cock. "Oh, God," he groaned.

Sutter's cock nearly exploded as the images and desires from Josh suffused his mind. Until Kendall, he and Josh had never had any desire to touch each other in that way; but now, the image of Josh sucking on his cock drove away his last shred of restraint. Gasping, he pulled his fingers from Kendall's ass.

Kendall bit her lip, staring into Josh's stormy grey eyes. He reached down to her waist and immobilized her hips once more. "It's okay, baby," he murmured. Kendall buried her face in his chest, her nails biting into his biceps as Sutter drove his cock into her in one rapid, determined thrust.

"Yes," she sobbed, her voice catching. "Oh, God, yes." She tried to rock her hips, so that Josh's cock would move inside her pussy, but the force of Sutter's thrusts caused Josh to slip out if she rocked too vigorously. After having to clumsily guide him back into her a couple of times, interrupting Sutter's desperate rhythm, she gave up and simply enveloped him with her pussy, pressing herself down onto him until she could feel the tip of his cock trapped tight against her deepest tissues. Sutter's thrusts became deeper, faster, and Kendall could feel through the bond that it wasn't even necessary for her to move— pleasure flooded Josh as Sutter's cock massaged his through her intervening flesh.

It was better than she ever would have imagined. Taking them *both*. Feeling both their cocks hot and ripe inside her. Kendall sobbed again, needing to come, but wanting to prolong this feverish ecstasy for as long as possible.

"Yes, Sutter," Josh groaned. "Fuck her. Fuck her." He gasped as Sutter's pace increased, feeling the friction against his cock through the flesh between. "Fuck *me!*" he roared.

Sutter pumped like a piston. "Oh, God," Kendall moaned, borne up on the crest of their bestial desire. "God, yes!" The three of them screamed in unison as their bodies froze, three sets of muscles, tendons and sinews paralyzed by passionate release. Kendall's anal and vaginal muscles contracted violently against the firm flesh imbedded within her, and warmth pervaded her body as Josh and Sutter's cocks pulsed in unison, filling her with their essence.

When he could, Sutter backed away and stood on trembling legs, then collapsed beside them on the bed. He reached out and stroked Kendall's hair, Josh's bicep. Josh opened his arm, and Sutter moved in close, the muscles in Josh's arm like steel against his back. Kendall's soft palm caressed him, her fingers feathering down his spine. He shivered.

Exhausted, they lay wrapped in each other's arms and drifted into satisfied, dreamless sleep.

Chapter Eight
Male Bonding

Kendall opened her eyes to find Josh sleeping and Sutter watching them both. Smiling, Kendall pushed herself off Josh and lay to his left, with Sutter to his right. Sutter's eyes ran the length of Josh's hard, lean body, coming to rest on his groin. A sense of desire and curiosity feathered through their connection. Josh moaned softly in his sleep. Sutter sought Kendall's gaze, his blue eyes hot with passion, his brow furrowed with uncertainty.

"What do you want?" Kendall asked him.

"I want Josh," he said. "I can't believe it. This has never happened before. But now—" he rubbed at his face. "God, I want to make him come so bad."

"We're three, Sutter," Kendall said. "And he wants it, too; I know you felt that. It's crazy to think that the three of us can do this for a lifetime and the two of you will never desire each other. Never touch each other. It's too intense."

"It's just—we fought people's perception of us as gay for so long. Why do I want it now?"

"Maybe because our soul is finally whole. Mated, in a sense. It doesn't seem strange that the two of you would want to make that mating a physical act as well." She propped her head up on one hand and grinned wickedly. "The three of us, actually, because the idea of the two of you joining the way we have makes me horny as hell."

Just voicing the thought made her nipples harden and she glanced down. Sutter followed her gaze and grinned, tweaking one teasingly. Kendall couldn't believe she was saying these things, but it just didn't feel wrong. Not in their situation.

Experimentally, Sutter reached out and drew his fingers along Josh's limp cock. Josh sighed and shifted restlessly, his eyes moving rapidly behind his eyelids. Sutter crooked his left elbow, supporting his head while he explored Josh's cock. He ran his fingers over the broad vein running its length, then fingered the ridge of the circumcision, watching. Josh moaned softly as his body began to respond, filling and firming beneath Sutter's hand. Sutter wrapped his fingers around the rigid flesh and began massaging as he moved down the length of Josh's cock.

"Mmmm." Josh opened his eyes. Sutter met his gaze as he took one of Josh's balls in his hand, squeezing slightly as he pulled it; then captured the other and repeated the movement, like milking an udder. Josh's breath quickened. Sutter raised his eyebrows questioningly. Josh swallowed; nervous, yet highly aroused. Before Kendall, he had never even thought of having intimate relations with Sutter, but now—he drew in a shaky breath at the fire developing in his loins. *God.* It surprised him, how much he wanted it.

"Josh?" Sutter prompted.

"Yes," Josh whispered hoarsely, answering the unspoken question.

Bees buzzed in his stomach as Sutter milked his cock, gently at first, then more firmly as his own desire grew. His touch was so different from Kendall's. Kendall's skin was soft, and even her tightest grip was nowhere near as snug as Sutter's. And her ministrations were tender. Coaxing. Sutter was vigorous. Demanding. Kendall's palm glided over his rod smoothly, whereas Sutter's rough callouses added another dimension of sensation. It wasn't necessarily *better*, just very different, and definitely erotic in its own way. He moaned involuntarily, and Sutter chuckled softly.

"You like that?" he asked. Josh's cheeks flushed, and he looked away, but nodded.

Just watching them made Kendall's nipples burn and her crotch throb, but she didn't want to intrude upon these first explorations. She reached down, slipping her middle finger into her pussy, rubbing her clit with her thumb as she observed avidly.

Sutter felt a deep sense of satisfaction as Josh's cock continued to lengthen and thicken with each stroke. A rush of desire filled his loins, and he shifted on the bed, bringing his mouth to the flushed head. A drop of semen glistened at its tip and Sutter licked it off roughly. Josh's body jerked. Sutter sent Josh an image of himself taking Josh's cock deep into his throat. "Yes," Josh groaned. His projected desire burned through Sutter like wildfire, and he groaned as well, surrounding Josh with his lips as his own cock began to lift and extend.

Gently at first, he began moving his lips up and down Josh's prick, sucking lightly. "God," Josh moaned, arching his hips. Excitement building, Sutter intensified his efforts. "Yes," Josh urged, a catch in his voice. "Damn, yes!" Sutter had been holding back somewhat, uncharacteristically tentative in this new situation, but with Josh's vocal demonstrations of pleasure, his natural impatience and enthusiasm took over. He pressed his lips tight against

Josh's hot flesh, allowing his teeth to scrape the skin slightly, sucking harder.

"Yes, damn it! Suck!" Josh commanded. Sutter devoured him, until Josh's cock became tender, raw, but the slight pain only served to elevate his need. Josh closed his eyes, concentrating on each sensation. His hands spasmed, gripping the covers. "Harder!" he cried. Sutter complied, sucking so hard, so demandingly, Josh could swear his nuts were going to emerge from the tip of his throbbing rod. "God! Yes." Josh bucked like a bronco, thrusting himself deep into Sutter's throat with each word. "Yes!"

Kendall gasped, Josh's outburst intensifying her own need as she plunged her finger in and out of her pussy. She glanced at Sutter and saw that his cock had swelled, bright droplets glistening on its tip. Moaning, she abandoned her self-stimulation and lay across Josh's legs, taking Sutter's distended shaft into her eager mouth.

Sutter convulsed as Kendall's warm, wet lips enveloped him. She began tonguing him urgently, circling his shaft with her thumb and forefinger, lapping at his seepage as she ran those fingers up and down his cock, twisting them back and forth as she went. Sutter moaned.

Josh's breath caught as the sound Sutter made vibrated through his shaft. He was vaguely aware of Kendall lying across his thighs, and opened his eyes. She was licking Sutter's dick ravenously as she jacked him off with her fingers. Her hips rested against Josh's left thigh, her leg cocked, giving him an enticing view of her glistening pussy. He reached out and buried his thumb between her red lips, capturing her clit between his forefinger and middle finger and squeezing.

The visual stimulation of watching them together had driven Kendall to a fever pitch before she ever took Sutter in her mouth. The fierce, demanding pleasure radiating from him, coupled with the surprised yet erotically charged emotions she was feeling from Josh had her balanced precariously on the brink of ecstasy. The addition of Josh's touch was too much, and Kendall's orgasm exploded before she had any chance to hold it back.

The sensation of Kendall's sudden, forceful climax hit Josh and Sutter through their mental bond like a wall, and Josh's cock spewed. Sutter choked and started to back off, but then purposefully clamped his lips against Josh's pulsing flesh and forced himself to swallow. The immediate, shocked gratitude that flowed into him from Josh almost triggered his own eruption. Desperately, he struggled to drink the last of Josh's semen before releasing him and pushing Kendall away to keep himself from jetting into her greedy mouth. She made a face, but when he sent her an image of his cock buried between Josh's lips her brow cleared and she nodded.

As soon as Josh's orgasm had passed Sutter sat up, then leaned over and kissed his lips. Reluctantly at first, Josh opened his mouth. Sutter's tongue danced over his lips, his teeth, even explored the space under his tongue, and the taste of his own semen was just as arousing in Sutter's mouth as it had been in Kendall's. Without conscious thought, he responded, returning Sutter's passion with his own. Sutter moaned and pulled back. "My turn." He grasped Josh's head with both hands and pulled it toward his crotch.

Josh resisted. "Wait a minute." His eyes twinkled. He nudged Kendall, motioning for her to move to the end of the bed, then pressed Sutter back into the pillows. "Close your eyes," he commanded, and sat back on his heels, waiting.

Sutter liked being in control. He liked knowing what was coming next. He tried to read Josh's intentions through the bond, but he was deliberately masking his thoughts. Kendall wouldn't be able to do it yet, having only been exposed to the bond for a few days, but Josh and Sutter had lived with the silent communication for so long that they could now — not sever it, but clutter their minds with extraneous information or images in order to bury something briefly. Josh didn't want him to know what he had planned. Sutter smiled ruefully. After years of being in control, he was being asked to sit back and let Josh take charge. He met Josh's gaze. It was hard to do, but he gave in and closed his eyes. At this point, his craving for the other man was so strong. Giving him the blowjob had only heightened his need. He was willing to do just about anything to feel Josh's touch.

Josh turned to Kendall, whispering in her ear. Her eyes widened, but she nodded. She slid from the bed and stood watching as he covered his hands with lubricant and began kneading Sutter's balls. "Oh, yeah," Sutter murmured. Josh dribbled the slick oil onto Sutter's groin, rolling the long cock between his hands as he smeared on a thick layer. "Mmmm," Sutter moaned. "I like that." Josh grinned to himself, then got up on all fours. He crawled upward until his hands were to either side of Sutter's shoulders and his knees straddled Sutter's waist. He nodded to Kendall, and she picked up the lubricant and squirted it onto his buttocks.

Kendall licked her lips. Moving closer, she imitated Sutter's earlier example and parted Josh's butt cheeks, placing the tip of the bottle just inside Josh's anus. He trembled with the effort of holding back a satisfied moan as the slippery fluid jetted into his canal. When she removed the tip, he almost cried out.

Sutter twitched, and Josh looked down. Gleaming ovals of oil glistened on his lover's abdomen. Josh shifted his legs, lowering his penis to Sutter's stomach, rubbing it over the slick unguent. "Mmmm." Sutter arched his back, and the tip of his cock prodded Josh's testicles. Josh moved back a little, until his cock was even with Sutter's, then began rubbing it briskly up and down the length of Sutter's erection. "Fuck." Sutter said. "Fuck! That's—" At a loss for words, Sutter made his feelings known through the bond. Sheer pleasure sizzled along Josh's nerve endings, making his manhood ache with longing. Kendall felt it as well, gasping at the intensity. Josh's legs trembled slightly as he raised himself again. He turned his head, his gaze urgent. Kendall squirted lubricant onto her hand, greasing it well, then reached out and parted Josh's cheeks.

"Oh!" he burst out involuntarily as Kendall pierced his ass with two fingers at once. Quick and efficient, she twisted her fingers back and forth, stretching him. Josh dipped his head and Sutter jumped involuntarily as his lover's tongue tickled his nipple. Josh moved his hips insistently, and Kendall parted her fingers slightly to insert the tip of a third digit.

"Hurry!" Josh groaned against Sutter's breast. Finding less resistance than she had expected, Kendall plunged that finger into him, moving all three digits in and out with a rapid twisting motion. "Oh, damn," he raised his head, breathing hard. Sutter's eyelids fluttered. "Keep them closed," Josh insisted hoarsely. With a final twist, Kendall removed her fingers. Reaching down, she grasped

Sutter's cock and held it steady. Josh sat up. Grabbing his butt-cheeks, he pulled them apart, then lowered himself. Kendall guided the tip of Sutter's cock to the slightly distended pink pucker of Josh's anus. Taking a deep breath, he sheathed Sutter's long, narrow rod with his ass.

Josh and Sutter both gasped, Sutter's eyes flying open. Josh watched him anxiously. "Oh, yeah!" Sutter growled, looking Josh boldly in the eyes. "Let me fuck you," he said. Demanding. Challenging. He reached up and grabbed Josh's shoulders, pushing against him as he rammed his cock deeper.

Josh's own eyes closed. God, it felt just as good for him as it had for Kendall. His ass was throbbing, begging for stimulation, and his cock had hardened again. Sutter was pulling at him now, trying to get him to begin the up-and-down motion, but there was something else Josh wanted. He sat up, gasping with unexpected pleasure as his repositioning allowed Sutter's staff to penetrate even farther. He held out a hand to Kendall.

She let him help her onto the bed, then straddled Sutter's waist, facing Josh. Lowering herself, she enfolded his cock with her warm, wet pussy. Josh groaned. Kendall was right. *Nothing* could compare with taking them both at the same time. With a wordless grunt, he used his powerful legs to pump himself up and down the length of Sutter's cock like doing squats in the gym, Kendall helping as best she could.

"Fuck!" Sutter yelled.

Kendall giggled. "We *are*," she pointed out.

"It's so good," Sutter murmured. "So *good!*" Sutter let his legs fall to either side, raising his hips to meet Josh's thrusts. "Damn," he gasped. "Yes!" Josh was taking him so deep, his cheeks pounded against Sutter's balls.

In this position, once again, Kendall wasn't really able to ride Josh properly. She moaned in frustration, knowing he would need more stimulation to come inside her.

Sutter picked up on the thought. *She's right.* He thought for a moment, then grinned. He reached out and slipped his hand between her buttocks, searching for her anus. "Mmmm." Kendall wriggled slightly, directing him to the tiny portal. Sutter slipped one finger into the channel, then another. Still supple and stretched from earlier, she took him easily. Experimentally, he probed with a third finger. It was tight, but he eased it in and out a few times. "Oh, God," Kendall moaned. Sutter pressed his fingers toward the back of Kendall's vaginal wall. Spreading them slightly, he pushed in until he could feel Josh's cock through her tissues. As Josh pumped Sutter's rod in and out of his ass, Sutter pressed hard. Through the intervening tissue, the two fingers to either side cradled Josh's cock, while his middle finger stroked the swollen vein running down its center.

"Yes. Yes!" Kendall and Josh cried in unison. With a low grunt, Sutter grasped Kendall's shoulder with his other hand and pushed, using her weight to bear Josh down, implanting his cock as deeply as possible in Josh's ass as his orgasm erupted and cum spewed.

Bone-melting warmth radiated out into Josh's body. Kendall threw back her head, moaning with delight as Sutter massaged Josh's pulsating prick with the tissues of her vagina. Her body shuddered as she came. Groaning, Josh climaxed as well. "Oh, God. Yes! Damn!" Sutter let go of Kendall's shoulder and grasped the sheets as Josh's anal contractions wrung his cock dry.

* * * * *

Kendall woke to find herself in a tangle of arms and legs, sheets damp with sweat and the scent of sex permeating the room. Inhaling deeply, she smiled to herself. She had never felt as relaxed and happy as she did now. She wished humans were capable of purring—it was such a perfect expression of contentment.

She carefully extricated herself from the pile on the bed and limped into the bathroom. Closing the door, she caught a glimpse of herself in the full-length mirror hanging at its back. Short legs, thick thighs, an even thicker belly. For a brief moment, she wondered again how two men built like Josh and Sutter could be interested in a woman of her size, but then she remembered their pricks pulsing inside her; the shivers of enjoyment that ran through the bond every time they touched her. She smiled with satisfaction. She had always told herself she was comfortable with her body, but realized that had never actually been true until now.

Turning to the shower, she leaned over and turned on the water, adjusting until it was just the way she liked it. Stepping in, she winced. Every muscle in her body was sore. She couldn't believe how many times they had made love this weekend. She wondered to herself if living with them was really a good idea. The distraction of having them near might mean that she and Sutter would never get any work done, Josh might never finish college. She laughed. Of course, the novelty would wear off eventually. This was so new to all of them, it was natural that they would revel in it—wallow in it, really. *Two lovers*, she thought. She never would have imagined such a life for herself, but it felt so *right*. Not for the first time, she wondered if the situation could ever possibly work on a long-term basis. She pushed the thought aside. She was damn well going to enjoy it. Forever, if possible. If not, then for as long as it lasted.

The warm water felt good, soothing her sore crotch and loosening aching muscles. Afterward, clean and dry, she crept into the darkened bedroom and grabbed her bag, taking it back into the bathroom with her so that she could dress. When she was finished, she went to the bed and stared down at her soul mates. They had moved together in her absence, and lay wrapped in each other's arms. Bending, she kissed each of their cheeks. Sutter's eyes opened. "What is it?" he asked.

"I have to go," Kendall whispered, not wanting to wake Josh. "I've got a sketch to finish for a client who's coming in tomorrow morning, and there are some things I need to do at the apartment."

He reached up and pulled her down, into a long, lingering kiss. Reluctantly, she drew away. "Really, Sutter. I have to go."

He sighed. "When are you moving in?"

Kendall's brow furrowed. "I'm not sure. We'll talk about it tomorrow, okay?"

"Okay." He thought for a moment. "Meet us for lunch?"

Kendall nodded agreement and backed away, her bag and purse in hand. "I'll see you tomorrow," she whispered. She blew him a kiss from the door, and headed downstairs. She called for a cab, then locked the front door behind her and waited on the porch until it arrived.

Chapter Nine
Breathless

On Monday, Kendall left the shop at eleven and drove up to the college. She scanned the parking lot until she spotted Sutter's convertible, then parked and walked over to wait beside it. Morning classes ended and the grounds filled with students. Kendall watched appreciatively as Sutter and Josh approached the car. *Damn, they really are drop-dead gorgeous*, she thought. Josh greeted her with a passionate kiss and stood with his arm around her. Kendall noticed several students watching, a speculative look in their eyes.

Sutter looked around briefly before planting a chaste kiss on Kendall's cheek. He blushed slightly as she raised her eyebrows quizzically.

"You call that a kiss?" Kendall laced the fingers of one hand in his short, fine hair and kissed him thoroughly, aware of staring eyes but not caring.

Sutter cleared his throat self-consciously and looked around again as she drew away, his face still flushed.

"You're all right with this, right?" Kendall asked. "I mean, we're going to be open about this relationship even in public, aren't we?"

Sutter nodded, but grimaced. "Yeah. It's just that I haven't had a chance to talk to my dad yet." He met Kendall's gaze. "I'd like for him to find out from me — not from the rumor mill."

That made sense. "Sorry," Kendall apologized. "I wasn't thinking."

Sutter shook his head. "No problem." He unlocked the car and opened the passenger door for her. "I guess I'm just used to hiding things." He grasped her hand, communicating silently. Kendall took a moment to examine the various feelings—a wave of happiness and certainty regarding the decision to live as a committed trio and to pursue his art overlaid a dark current of apprehension over quitting school and his anxiety about telling his father.

"It's all right, I understand." Kendall slid into the seat. She tried to radiate confidence and reassurance, though she was secretly concerned by the amount of discordance thoughts of his father seemed to generate in Sutter.

Sutter shut the door and walked around to the driver's side. While he got into the car, Josh stepped up. "I can't come to lunch," he said. "I've got to finish a project for fall finals." Kendall felt her disappointment wash through the bond. "I'm sorry. I'll make it up to you tonight." He bent and brought his lips to hers in a long, lingering embrace that left her breathless. When he finally pulled away, he was grinning.

"Wow!" Kendall ran a hand through her hair.

"We *will* see you tonight?"

Kendall nodded. "Why don't you both come to my place?" Both men nodded, then Josh glanced at his watch. "I've got to go—I reserved mainframe time and they'll give it away if I'm late. I'll see you later." He turned and walked quickly toward the Computer Science building.

Sutter stuck his keys in the ignition. "What sounds good for lunch?"

Kendall shrugged. "I don't know Houston very well. Any suggestions?"

"There's this place called *Jenny's*. They have great seafood."

Kendall smiled. "Sounds great. I could go for some shrimp."

Sutter nodded and pulled out of the parking lot. At the restaurant, Sutter asked for a table outside so that they could talk privately. "This weekend was amazing," he told Kendall while they were waiting for their orders to come.

Kendall smiled. "Yes it was."

Sutter slipped his right foot out of his shoe and worked his sock off. After the waiter brought their food, he nibbled at his fries while he watched Kendall attack her shrimp with gusto. Noticing his attention, she seemed embarrassed. "Speaking of this weekend, I worked up quite an appetite."

Sutter shook his head and grinned. "Hey, I *like* people who enjoy their food." He picked up his soda and sipped, then enquired idly, "What are you wearing under that dress?"

Kendall's breath caught in her throat. That morning when dressing, she had done something she'd never done before. She glanced at him through her eyelashes. "Nothing," she admitted hoarsely.

Sutter looked around. There were no other people eating on the deck, probably because the temperature was only in the sixties and the sky was overcast, threatening rain. His eyes dark with desire, he scooted his chair close to the small table, then lifted her skirt with his bare foot.

Kendall met his gaze, moving her own chair closer to the table. Reaching down, she crab-walked her fingers down her thighs, pulling the skirt up and over her knees, parting her legs slightly. Sutter's toes found her clit, and he rubbed them back and forth across it. "Mmmm," Kendall hummed under her breath. Sutter turned his foot a bit and slid his big toe into her wet pussy. "Yes," Kendall breathed, parting her legs farther and scooting her hips forward. Sutter flexed his toe, wiggling it back and forth inside her. "Oh, yes," Kendall murmured. Grasping the seat of her chair with her hands, she clenched her pussy.

"Oh, yeah." It was Sutter's turn to moan. He met her gaze. "I like how strong your pussy is."

Kendall clenched her muscles again as Sutter's toe wriggled inside her. "Oh, man," he murmured. Kendall felt her cheeks flushing as desire rose inside her. Sutter smiled and flexed his toes up and down, the smaller ones grazing Kendall's clitoris enticingly.

"Yes," Kendall moaned. She kept her eyes locked on his as she flexed and relaxed her vaginal muscles.

"Refill?" Kendall jumped as the waiter appeared behind her, tea pitcher in hand. Sutter's gaze trapped hers as she nodded wordlessly and waited while the man filled her glass and walked away. A shiver of wicked pleasure crawled down her spine.

"Let's eat," Sutter insisted. "This food's too good to let it go to waste."

Kendall groaned, but followed Sutter's example and continued eating. It was incredibly erotic, eating with Sutter's toe buried inside her. As she ate, the heat in her pelvis increased.

Their lunch became a series of short silences, punctuated occasionally by Kendall's soft gasps as Sutter flexed within her, and Sutter's wordless groans when her pussy clasped him tightly.

When they were finished, Sutter withdrew his foot and pulled on his sock and shoe. "What—" Kendall started, but Sutter hushed her. He picked up their ticket and held out his hand.

Ensconced in Sutter's convertible, they headed back to the college. "I guess I was putting it off," Sutter said. "I actually went to classes this morning." His voice filled with resolve. "But I'm going to go ahead and withdraw this afternoon."

"You know," Kendall said, "You don't have to quit school this minute. You're only six and a half months from having a bachelor's degree. If you want to wait, I'm okay with that."

Sutter glanced at her. "Are you sure?"

Kendall nodded. "I don't want you to do anything hasty—throw away three and a half years of work. I just want you to be happy."

"Well, I *would* like to finish my B.A. If this artist thing doesn't work out, I may need it."

"That's fine," Kendall rested a hand on his thigh. "I just don't want you to end up trapped in a job you *hate*."

Sutter covered her hand in his, flooding her with warmth and love.

When they had parked, Sutter reached to open the door, but was stopped by Kendall's hand on his thigh. He looked at her.

"Please, Sutter." Her thighs were wet with her juices and her pussy ached for his touch. "I need to come."

"Tonight," Sutter promised, and Kendall whimpered. He captured her chin in his hand and met her gaze as he allowed the sensation of throbbing tightness in his member to flow through their bond. "Just think how good it's going to be," he whispered. "Tonight."

"Oh, God," Kendall said. Her voice shook, but she nodded. "All right."

Sutter kissed her briefly, then got out of the car and came around to open her door. A shock of pleasure ripped through him when Kendall kissed his groin right before she stood. She grinned wickedly at the sudden lust that filled his eyes. "Tonight," she whispered, and kissed his cheek before she turned and headed for her car.

* * * * *

"So what do you think?" Kendall asked Brandy as she finished framing a pair of commissioned watercolor selkies for a customer who was coming by that evening.

"I'd *love* to have the apartment," Brandy admitted, studying her friend carefully over the pile of receipts she was tallying. "But are you sure about this?"

"I've never been so sure of anything in my life." Kendall tapped the final finishing nail into place. She cleaned the glass with alcohol and held one up. "Perfect?"

Brandy scrutinized the mat, frame and glass. "Perfect," she agreed. Kendall stepped over to the workbench and began wrapping the piece carefully.

Brandy was watching with wide eyes. "It just floors me, that's all. I knew they were different, but this business of soul mates and all—" She shook her head. "I don't understand it, but if it makes you happy…"

"It does," Kendall insisted. Her smile lit up her face. "I can't describe what it's like, but when you meet that one guy for you, you'll understand." She thought for a moment, then added teasingly, "Or two!"

Brandy raised her eyebrows scoffingly, but bit back a sarcastic retort. She thought Kendall was fooling herself thinking something like this could work, but the woman was her best friend. Brandy would support her for as long as it lasted, and be there to help Kendall pick up the pieces afterward. She sighed. "When can I move in?"

"I've already paid the mortgage for this month and December," Kendall mused. "But I'd rather be out there. If you want, we could make the move this weekend, and you wouldn't have to make your first payment until January the first."

"I couldn't do that," Brandy protested. "I can at least reimburse you for December."

Kendall shook her head. "Hey, you're doing me a favor, moving in on such short notice. Consider it your Christmas bonus!"

Brandy grinned. "Okay, okay. You don't have to twist *my* arm. I can't wait to have an apartment to myself!"

Kendall hugged Brandy impulsively. "I'm so *happy*," she crowed. Brandy returned the hug, but frowned to herself as Kendall sailed away to greet a customer.

* * * * *

Sutter and Josh sauntered into the shop around five-thirty that evening. "Hi!" Kendall came around the counter and met them with a peck on the lips. Brandy walked up behind them and Kendall waved toward her. "I think you know Brandy?"

"Sure." Sutter smiled at her friend and Josh nodded his head.

"She's going to go ahead and move into the apartment this weekend," Kendall informed them. "If that's okay."

Josh's eyes glittered as he met her gaze. "That's perfect," he said. "I was hoping we wouldn't have to wait too long."

Brandy rolled her eyes behind their backs and Kendall made a face at her.

"Anyway, we thought we'd come get the key and wait for you upstairs," Sutter explained.

"Just a sec." Kendall walked back to the office and came out with her keys. "Here you go. I'll be up a little after eight."

Sutter took the key and turned to go, waving to Brandy as he and Josh walked out the door. Brandy stood next to Kendall and watched them go. "Damn," she murmured. "I'd forgotten how hot they are." She cast a sly glance up at her friend. "You *go*, girl!"

Kendall chuckled. For the next couple of hours it was hard to keep her mind focused and her nervous energy in check. After she had straightened every painting on the wall for about the fifth time, Brandy groaned. "Why don't you go ahead and *go* already?"

Kendall glanced at the clock. Seven-thirty. "Are you sure?"

Brandy snagged Kendall's sweater off the hook next to the office and handed it to her, pushing her toward the door. "I'm sure. I can lock up by myself."

"Thanks, Brandy. I owe you one."

Brandy nodded. "You can buy me lunch tomorrow. And I want details, woman. Details!"

Kendall grinned and swept out the door. She hurried around to the back and rushed up the stairs, then paused for a minute to catch her breath before she walked into the apartment.

A cheerful fire crackled in the fireplace and the spicy aroma of spaghetti sauce made her stomach rumble. She tossed her sweater onto a recliner and went into the kitchen.

Josh stood at the stove stirring while Sutter was just finishing up draining the pasta. He looked around as she walked in. "Hey!"

Kendall took a deep breath. "This smells wonderful, guys. Thanks." She walked over and hugged Josh's back, breathing in the musky scent of his cologne. Sutter dumped the pasta into a bowl and came over for a quick kiss.

"Why don't you go wait in the living room?" he suggested. "We'll be in when it's ready."

Kendall hesitated, used to doing for herself, but she could feel through the bond how much they enjoyed pampering her, so she turned and went into the living room. She sat on the couch and kicked off her shoes. The crackling fire, clatter of dishes from the kitchen and occasional murmur of conversation filled Kendall with a deep sense of contentment. When they came out, she was lying on the couch, her eyes half-closed.

"Wake up, sleepyhead," Sutter nudged her foot. Kendall sat up and watched in puzzlement as Josh pushed back the coffee table and spread a canvas painter's cloth over the floor.

"What are you doing?"

They both ignored her, bringing in hot pads and dishes from the kitchen and placing them on the coffee table. When they were finished, Sutter held out his hand and helped Kendall up from the couch. Without a word, he reached back and began unzipping her dress.

"Sutter—" Kendall began, but he silenced her with a toe-curling kiss. Her dress fell down around her ankles. Sutter stepped back.

"Take it off," he commanded. Kendall unfastened her bra and let it slide to the floor. Bending, she picked up her dress and tossed the items onto the couch. She had to fight the urge to cover herself with her hands as her lovers stood there, drinking in the sight of her.

Sutter grinned. "Let's eat."

Kendall sat cross-legged on the canvas. Josh dished up a bowl of spaghetti and sauce and handed it to Kendall. Self-consciously, she began eating, wincing when a loop of pasta escaped her mouth and trailed sauce down her chin. She sucked in the errant ribbon and looked around for a napkin. "Let me get that for you," Josh said. Leaning over, he nibbled the sauce from her chin, making his way up to her lips for a taste of spicy tongue.

"Aren't the two of you going to eat?"

"After you," Josh insisted. Kendall shook her head, but kept on eating, growing more aroused with every minute. Their gaze on her flushed nipples was like a caress, making each peak even more pronounced; and when they focused on her furry crotch, it was all she could do to keep from touching herself to alleviate her need.

As she finished the last bite and set her empty bowl on the table, Kendall's body ached with desire. "Why don't you lie down?" Sutter suggested. Swallowing hard, Kendall reclined between them on the tarp. Reaching out, Josh lifted her knees and spread her legs, positioning her so that her swollen red pussy was easily accessible.

"Breadstick?" Josh offered. Sutter nodded and accepted the hard, cigar-shaped object he offered. He took a bite and shook his head. "Needs something," he murmured. Kendall moaned as he reached between her legs and dipped the breadstick's tip in and out of her pussy several times. Her natural lubrication trickled down, tickling the valley between the swell of her buttocks. Capturing her gaze, he ate the portion he had moistened, then penetrated her again. Kendall felt her juices gush as her pussy spasmed. Sutter smiled. "Mmmm, you're so wet." He brought the stick up to his mouth and ate the rest. "I love the way you taste." Electric tremors shot through her at his words.

Kendall watched silently as Josh grabbed a breadstick and knelt between her spread legs. He slid the appetizer between her slick lips. Kendall moaned. With his thumb, he pushed the object deep inside her, until only a small portion protruded. He lowered his face to her crotch. Kendall brought herself up on her elbows so she could see past her tummy. His gaze locking with hers, Josh nipped at the end of the breadstick, causing it to tremble erratically inside her. "Mmmm." Kendall wiggled her hips. Josh caught the bread between his teeth and backed it out, then slid it in, swirling his tongue around its circumference when he had it buried again. "Oh, God." Kendall's eyes blazed as he began wiggling the stick with his teeth, occasionally slipping his tongue in and licking. Slowly, he worked his way down the breadstick, eating as he went. With each soft cry she uttered, his cock hardened further and his desire increased. He reached between her swollen lips with his thumbs, pulling them as far apart as he could. He brought the final bite into his mouth, watching, nibbling her juicy crevices as he chewed. Her bright eyes clouded, became unfocused. As her breathing quickened, he swallowed and plunged his tongue into her warm gulf. Kendall dropped her head back and arched as one wave of ecstasy after another washed through her. Josh's cock throbbed as her pussy clenched rapidly on his tongue. When it was over, she lay back on the tarp, sighing in contentment.

"Mmmm," Josh murmured. "I love how that feels on my tongue."

Kendall moaned, her entire body fired with need. Sutter fixed himself a bowl of pasta, stirring it to coat each ribbon with the thick sauce. With his fingers, he withdrew a few strands and trailed them across Kendall's breasts, drawing crazy red trails over her areoles. Then he settled the strands atop one breast, looping them round and round her nipple. Bending over, he caught the tail end of one with his lips, sucking it from her. Each loop grazed her ripe bud, until the tip was tingling. Her breathing grew ragged. "You like that?" Sutter asked. Kendall nodded. As he began to repeat the process with a second strand, Josh trailed his own handful over her other nipple, down between her breasts, over her belly. He tickled the interior of her belly button with one strand, then continued on. Lifting up her belly, he reached out and dipped the strands in the sauce again, and drew them across the curve where her tummy segued into her abdomen. Kendall shivered involuntarily.

Sutter sucked the last strand from her right breast and sat up. Josh lifted each breast and decorated the curve at its base. That done, he reached down. Kendall gasped as he tucked the strands inside her pussy.

In unison, he and Sutter bent and began cleaning her breasts, licking and laving, sucking her nipples as she gasped and moaned. Lifting each mound, they licked the sensitive curve beneath, peppering her with kisses, making her cry out with need. Sutter claimed her mouth. "So beautiful." He nuzzled her neck. "We're going to memorize every inch." He nibbled on her earlobe, sending shivers down her spine. "Find all your secret places," he whispered. Kendall turned her head and kissed him urgently, rousing heat in his groin with her passion.

Kendall started as Josh's tongue dipped into her belly button, teasing and twirling. He and Sutter began nipping lightly at her tummy, following the erratic red trails. "Oh, God," Kendall murmured. Josh lifted her belly and they both began sucking spices from the place where her stomach joined her groin. "Oh, God," Kendall mumbled again, shocked when goosebumps traveled down her pelvis, into her bush. She hadn't known that was possible. She drowned in a river of pleasure as they kissed and nibbled their way through her damp curls to the dark cavern beneath. Kendall spread her legs wide as they moved between them.

Josh caught a loop of spaghetti with his tongue and slowly sucked the tendril from her vagina, tugging occasionally when there was gentle resistance. Kendall moaned and thrashed above him. Sutter leaned in and followed his example.

Kendall arched her back and gasped. Her nipples throbbed, hard and ripe. Moaning, she brought her hands up and grasped them between thumb and forefingers, rolling the hard nubs faster and faster as Sutter and Josh pleasured her pussy. She felt the last strand slip free, and then they were both inside her; their tongues tasting her, dancing with one other, tasting her again. Kendall cried out as she came again.

Kendall rested, panting, for several minutes. When she opened her eyes, they were watching her with satisfied smiles. Kendall grinned back and sat up. "My turn," she said seductively. She reached out and pushed against their chests, urging them to stretch out on the floor. Then she got up and went into the kitchen. They could hear her rummaging through drawers. In a moment, she returned with a pastry brush. She sat cross-legged between them, the bowl of sauce cradled in her lap. Her eyes smoldering, she began brushing the thick, spicy mixture onto their stiff shafts, over their balls, along the sensitive ridge that traveled from the base of their cocks to their anus.

Josh closed his eyes as her mouth engulfed one of his testicles. Sutter reached out and grabbed his hand, and Josh squeezed hard as she sucked, her tongue swirling round and round. Sutter shivered as Josh's sensations rippled through the bond. Kendall radiated pleasure as she felt their responses. She switched, capturing one of Sutter's balls between her lips. She nipped lightly with her teeth, wanting to please him, knowing he liked things a little rougher.

Sutter gasped when he felt that thought, sensed how much she wanted to please him. He groaned, tangling one hand in her hair, grasping her head and grinding her against him. "Oh, damn!" he cried out as she took the other sac into her mouth, sucking, pulling, kneading with her tongue. "Kendall, I can't—"

Kendall instinctively let go and wrapped her mouth around his cock. He thrust hard, burying himself against the back of her throat as his semen gushed. Kendall gagged a little, but did not back away, swallowing urgently as he thrashed against her.

"Damn," Sutter muttered shakily when it was over. "You are so *good*."

Kendall licked her lips seductively and leaned over, her breath hot on Josh's cock. "Mmmm," she murmured. "I'm still hungry." Josh whispered her name. With bold eyes, she sucked the sauce from the hair covering his groin, his testicles, dancing all around his swollen member, but not touching it.

"Kendall, please," he groaned. She brought her mouth close, her breath hot on his shaft. Then she blew lightly, the cool air somehow making his cock even more feverish. He moaned. She looked up at him.

"What, Josh?"

"God." He ran a hand through his ragged locks. "Suck me, Kendall."

Kendall ran her tongue lightly up his cock. "Are you sure?" she teased.

Groaning, he raised his hips, pressing his hot flesh against her lips. She kissed it, then took the flushed head in her mouth and swirled her tongue around and around. Then she took her lips away. "Please," he moaned. Kendall waited, eyes glittering. "Please, Kendall." He felt a thrill quiver through the bond. He sensed how much she liked knowing how desperately he wanted it, enjoyed that bit of power she had over him. His groin burned. That was fine with him. "Please, Kendall. Please," he begged for her, his eyes gleaming, enjoying her pleasure. "Please suck me. Please."

Kendall teased the tip of his penis with her tongue, letting the waves of his urgent need wash over her. Finally, Kendall walked her lips down, allowing his thick, steely shaft to fill her mouth.

Kendall felt Sutter's hands on her hips and raised them, resting on her knees, her butt in the air. She whimpered as his fingers penetrated her pussy, fast and furious. She increased her pace, plunging up and down on Josh's cock, trembling at the edge of orgasm, but wanting to come when he came.

Josh reveled in the feel of her. Her tongue circling his cock's thick diameter. Her curtain of silky tresses cascading over him, tickling his thighs. Kendall's rhythm faltered as intense pleasure flooded into him from her. Sutter had found her G-spot.

Kendall moaned over and over as Sutter fingered that secret place inside her, the vibrations humming through Josh's cock almost overwhelming his control. Sutter reached out with his other hand, feathering his fingers across Kendall's back, from her shoulder blades to her upraised hips. Kendall shivered, goosebumps raising on her flesh.

Josh wrapped his hand around the back of Kendall's head, massaging her scalp as she licked and laved, occasionally groaning as she nipped the tip of his cock hungrily.

Kendall felt Sutter's fingers in her crack. She shifted slightly, thrusting her butt higher, excited by his touch. Then he switched hands, bringing the two fingers wet with her juices against her puckered anus. Kendall breathed in sharply through her nose as Sutter teased the tiny opening. She moaned, clenching Josh's cock tightly with her mouth, sucking hard. Sutter pushed a fraction of his finger into her tight canal. Kendall's stomach clenched as electric pulses of desire traveled from her anus to her pussy.

"Mmmm," she purred against Josh's cock. Sutter probed farther and farther, infiltrating the warm, narrow passage. Kendall moaned again. Sutter began wiggling his finger inside her. Kendall's vaginal juices welled.

A quick spurt of semen escaped from Josh's cock as he watched Sutter's finger disappear deep inside Kendall's ass. He managed to keep from losing control, holding on as he watched Sutter finger-fuck her ass and her pussy, as her movements on his cock became more and more insistent.

Kendall swallowed Josh's leakage eagerly, moaning repeatedly. She quickened her pace, plumbing her mouth with Josh's cock, sucking as hard as she could. "Yes!" he exclaimed. Sutter abandoned all restraint and buried his fingers deep inside her pussy while he relentlessly plumbed her ass. Kendall drove her hips into him as Josh shuddered and pushed her down, planting his cock against the back of her throat. "God, Kendall, yes!"

A tide of semen streamed into her throat, and Kendall feasted on his seething juices. Sutter froze as Josh's orgasm washed over him, almost as pleasurable as having one himself. He continued dipping into Kendall's anus with his long, slender finger, prodding her ever higher on the crest of her orgasm. When she had drunk all Josh had to give, Kendall let go of his cock and arched her back, screaming Sutter's name as she swept over the peak, every nerve in her body swamped by overwhelming pleasure.

She collapsed on the damp canvas, breathing hard and covered in sweat. "Oh, God," Kendall moaned. Josh couldn't move, feeling as though his bones had melted in the heat of their climax.

"Are you all right?" Sutter asked.

Kendall shook her head. "I'm drowning."

He cupped her face in his hand. "What do you mean?"

"Being apart from the two of you is like being deprived of air. I can't wait to see you again. But when you're with me, it's so intense I feel like I'm drowning." She couldn't meet his gaze. "Either way, I can't breathe."

Sutter loomed over her, his mouth hovering inches from hers. He beckoned to Josh. "Breathe *us*," he whispered. Capturing her gaze, he breathed out. Heart pounding, Kendall breathed in, taking the warm, moist air into her lungs. She breathed out, and Sutter breathed in. He leaned back and Josh took his place, breathing out. Kendall stared into his eyes as they breathed one another. Heat flooded her chest, her breasts. Josh's fingers crept down her abdomen. Kendall's breath caught in her throat as he thrust his thumb and middle finger into her pussy. She tried to push him away. "Not again." She shook her head. "I can't-"

"Yes, you can." He swirled his finger around, then slipped it out, leaving his thumb implanted as he slid his finger down between her crack.

Kendall moaned and laced her hands behind his head, pulling his lips to hers, sucking at his tongue hungrily. She spread her legs, then untangled her fingers from his hair and reached down, grasping her own butt cheeks with her hands, pulling them apart for him. His finger slipped inside her anus. He broke off the kiss and sat up, wanting to see himself buried inside her.

Kendall uttered sobbing cries of delight as Josh embedded his fingers in her - probing, prodding, driving her wild. Thick juices oozed from her pussy with each plunge, seeping down along her crack, making it even easier for Josh to penetrate her. Kendall moaned and pushed herself up onto her elbows, trying to *see*.

Sutter immediately reached out and grasped her under her knees. He supported her back with his chest as he raised them into the air, until she had a perfect view of Josh's fingers inside her. "Yes!" Kendall gasped, watched avidly as Josh began rocking his hand back and forth, penetrating each hole alternately, his thumb in her pussy, his finger in her ass. "Oh, yes," Kendall moaned. Watching her pussy spasm with each penetration, her anus tighten and relax—it was incredibly erotic and extremely satisfying.

She felt the surge rising and squeezed her legs together tightly, trapping Josh's fingers inside her, gasping as both canals contracted over and over against the fingers buried inside them. "Oh, God," she moaned when it had passed and she was lying between her lovers. "How can I take this? It's too much!"

Sutter trapped her chin in his hand, turning her face to him. He shook his head. "No. It will never be *enough*." In unison, he and Josh reached down and their fingers took possession of her pussy again. Over and over, they brought her to climax. The world faded as Kendall rode wave after wave of violent ecstasy and lost herself to them.

Chapter Ten
Moving Day

Kendall woke the next morning to muscles that screamed in protest as she extricated herself from the arms of her lovers. She made her way on trembling limbs into the bathroom and turned on the water for a shower. As she stood beneath the wonderfully warm jets, she thought of the night before and felt her cheeks growing hot.

They had made her come over and over, reducing her to a quivering mass of desire begging for their touch. She had cried, it felt so good. Nothing in life should be that good. It was frightening. Every time she thought she had a handle on the relationship, something happened that made her question her sanity once more. *What have I gotten myself into?*

Don't do that! she told herself angrily as she lathered her hair. It was too late for second-guessing. *All right, so I'm scared. That's not surprising. When it's this good, there's even more to lose.* And that was the crux of the matter, she realized. The past few months, since the first time they entered her store, had a dream-like quality about them. She suddenly recognized that she was still waiting for the other shoe to drop.

And for some reason, just recognizing that fact made her feel better. Reality slipped into place, and Kendall's remaining doubts melted away. It was ridiculous to question any more whether this was the right thing for her. She had already made the commitment—she was moving in. She could feel Sutter and Josh's very *thoughts,* for God's sake! She knew without a doubt that they loved her. And she absolutely loved both of them, with every fiber of her being. As a matter of fact, she realized she could feel them even now, a presence in the back of her mind. Felt their consciousnesses stirring and knew they were waking up, and was gratified that their first coherent thoughts were of her.

When she had dressed and come out of the bedroom, breakfast was on the table. Josh and Sutter had already eaten. They gave her quick good-mornings and then headed in to shower and make themselves presentable for their morning classes. By the time she had finished and cleared off the table, they were ready to leave. She kissed them goodbye, receiving assurances that they would be back that evening. Apparently, they were prepared to stay in the apartment until she could move out to the house that weekend, which was fine with her.

* * * * *

Kendall was glad when the weekend finally arrived. Although the week would have dragged if the guys hadn't stayed with her, the apartment definitely wasn't big enough for three.

Brandy had purchased most of Kendall's furniture— which was primarily second-hand bargain finds anyway— for a reasonable price, as the house was fully furnished and Brandy had nothing but her bed. Kendall hung onto a few items which had sentimental value—the recliner that had belonged to her brother; a full-length antique mirror that he had given to her on her sixteenth birthday. So moving day actually ended up being moving morning.

Brandy borrowed a truck from one of her friends, and in two trips, they had all Kendall's stuff out at the house.

Josh and Sutter left to return the truck and Kendall stayed behind to begin putting things away. She was in the spare bedroom hanging up her clothes when she heard a car in the driveway. *The guys must be back.* She jogged downstairs and opened the door. A tall man was walking across the porch, probably in his late forties or early fifties, graying at the temples and with eyes like Sutter's.

He frowned. "I'm looking for Sutter."

"He ran into town for a minute," Kendall said. "Can I help you?" She held out her hand. "You're David Campbell, right?"

He shook her hand brusquely. "Right."

"Sutter favors you," Kendall observed.

David appeared irritated. "And you are—?"

"Oh, sorry. Kendall Aaronson." She opened the door and stood back. "Would you like to come in?"

David stepped over the threshold and looked around. Kendall's recliner and mirror were sitting in the entry, waiting for Sutter and Josh's return to be carried up the stairs into the guest bedroom. Kendall edged past them and led David Campbell into the living room. He gestured toward the furniture as they passed. "What's going on?"

Kendall was only slightly surprised to realize that Sutter had apparently still not spoken to his father. She wondered what to say, then shrugged internally and decided that she would be completely honest. "I'm moving in." She waved him to a chair and took a seat on the sofa.

"Oh." David sat and favored her with a calculating gaze. Weighing, measuring. "And do you belong to Sutter or Josh?"

Kendall almost laughed out loud. "Well, I don't *belong* to anyone. If you're asking exactly who I'm moving in with—both of them, actually."

Sutter's father appeared puzzled. "A roommate? Why? They don't need help with the house payment—I take care of that."

"Ummm, actually, Sutter was supposed to talk to you about that." Kendall straightened as David frowned. "That won't be necessary anymore. We've taken the liberty of changing the payment to a monthly bank draft from my account."

David's demeanor changed from puzzled condescension to immediate antagonism. "And why is that?" he demanded.

Kendall breathed in deeply and took the plunge. "We're—not a couple. A trio, I guess you could say. Josh and Sutter and I have a relationship. Something we intend to make permanent. And I'm in a position to support them both until they finish school."

David's face had reddened, and his brow furrowed with fury. "You're after his money, aren't you? You know Sutter's going to be a lawyer, you know he'll inherit my estate eventually, and you're going to ride his coattails to the payoff. Just like Josh."

Kendall bristled. "Okay, first of all, I have a successful business and don't *need* a man or his money. Second—if that were true, why would I be willing to take on all the bills you're currently paying? Third, Sutter's not going on to law school. He's going to finish his Bachelor's and—"

David jumped from the chair and towered over her. "Not going to law school!" he roared. "What the hell are you talking about? I paid for his college with the understanding that he is going to go on to Harvard and get his law degree. I pulled strings to get him accepted. He damned well *is* going to law school!"

David felt his heart pounding as he loomed over the girl. But she wasn't a girl, actually. She was a woman. She had to be at least thirty. What was she doing with Sutter and Josh? His mind reeled. He never lost control like this. He forced a deep breath, calming himself. The woman was looking up at him, composed with an infuriatingly amused smile twitching at her lips. He took a step back and forced his hands open, releasing the fists he hadn't even realized he'd formed.

"I'm sorry," Kendall said. "Sutter doesn't want to be a lawyer. He never has. He's going to finish his four-year degree and go into business for himself."

David felt his fingers curling in again and clasped his hands behind his back. "Doing what?" he asked roughly.

"Painting. Sketching. Carving." Kendall pointed to the banister. "Did you know all that is his work?"

David didn't even glance in that direction. "An artist. You're telling me he wants to be a frigging artist?" His voice dripped derision.

Kendall felt her ire rising, and fought to keep her own voice calm, though it came out a bit frosty. "Yes. And he'll do just fine."

David Campbell shook his head, eyes stormy, jaws clenched. "I don't know what you and Josh Reed have cooked up, but—"

Kendall rose abruptly. "I think you'd better leave now." She walked over to the front door and held it open.

David trembled with the effort of holding his temper in check. "You can't throw me out of this house. It's mine—I put the money down to get it built. I've been paying for it."

"And we'll pay you back. Eventually. But it's not your house. It's in Sutter and Josh's names; and in a few weeks, mine as well." David stared in disbelief. "Oh, and while I'm thinking about it—the car payment's taken care of as well. You don't have to give Sutter a single penny more."

David stalked toward her. "I don't believe a word of this. When I talk to Sutter—"

"You'll find out everything has changed," Kendall interrupted smoothly. "Mr. Campbell, let's understand each other right now. Sutter doesn't—" she searched for a word, then deliberately used the term David had implemented earlier, "*Belong* to you any more. He's a man, and he's going to make his own decisions and do what makes *him* happy."

She stood before him, and despite her lack of height, her confidence and determination somehow dominated the room. "I'm not afraid of you, Campbell. I think you've been manipulating Sutter his whole life. That's not going to happen any more."

"So now *you're* going to do it," David growled.

Kendall chuckled and shook her head. "If it pleases you to think that, so be it. But as a matter of fact, this wouldn't be happening so quickly if *you* weren't trying to use your money as leverage to force Josh out. The bottom line is that Sutter is going to live his own life from now on." She opened the door a bit wider. "I'm not your enemy, David, but I can be if you make it necessary."

David Campbell normally would have laughed at such a threat, but the woman was so damn unintimidated! And if she had really persuaded Sutter to add her name to the deed and to reject his financial support—"Do you know who I am?" he growled. "How much power I wield in this town?"

She looked him in the eye. "Frankly, I don't care."

And he could tell she meant it. For the first time in a long time, David Campbell found himself facing someone who wasn't afraid of him. Thrown off balance, he couldn't think of a single thing to say. Kendall took hold of his elbow and urged him over the threshold. "Goodbye, Mr. Campbell. Hopefully, you'll calm down in a couple of days and see that everything's going to be all right. It would be nice if you and Sutter could have a better relationship." Before he could tell her she knew nothing about his relationship with his son, she had shut the door in his face. He stormed off the porch and peeled down the driveway in a spray of dirt and gravel.

When Sutter and Josh had returned, and she had related everything that had happened, Sutter collapsed onto the couch and ran his hands through his hair. "God, Kendall. I'm sorry. I meant to tell him earlier this week, but I kept putting it off."

"No problem." Kendall sat on the couch next to him. She could feel his anxiety. Reaching up, she drew his head down to rest on her shoulder. "Trust me, Sutter. Everything is going to work out fine. It's just going to take some time."

Sutter closed his eyes. She radiated a steady flow of confidence and certainty, and he felt better. But he couldn't rid himself of a tiny knot of dread in the pit of his stomach. David Campbell didn't like to have his plans thwarted. And as much as Sutter would have liked to believe it, he didn't think his father was going to take this lying down.

Chapter Eleven
Promises to Keep

Kendall closed the shop for the week of Christmas, figuring any locals who were going to purchase their gifts from her had already done so, and the tourists had come and gone. Plus, Sutter and Josh were off for winter break. It was nice to stay home and spend the day with them. To bake pies and cookies, to plan a Christmas dinner.

There was a steady stream of friends out to visit. Sutter had a large group of acquaintances. Slowly, as he had become comfortable with the idea that he was out from under his father's control and didn't need to hide his real feelings any longer, he had revealed the true nature of their relationship to the people he trusted the most. A couple had been unable to deal with the knowledge and had simply started avoiding him. Most, however, as they saw how happy the trio was, were able to put aside their preconceptions and accept the three of them without question. Josh had even come out of his shell, as people made the effort to get to know him now that they realized how important he was to Sutter. Kendall had discovered that he had a very warm and generous soul and a wry sense of humor that people loved. But Brandy's circle of friends had been the best. Like herself, they had loving natures and open minds and welcomed Kendall and her unusual family into their group wholeheartedly.

The only dark cloud was David Campbell. He had spoken to Sutter only once, to find out if Kendall's assertions had been correct. When Sutter confirmed and refused to bow to his father's demands, David Campbell had hung up on him and they hadn't heard from him since. Kendall and Josh could both feel how much that was hurting Sutter despite the fact that the relationship had been so adversarial.

On Christmas Eve, the three of them lounged in their favorite spot—the rug in front of the fireplace—cuddling under a fleecy blanket. The clock on the mantel struck midnight. Sutter and Josh sat up abruptly, sharing a secretive glance.

"What are you guys up to?" Kendall asked suspiciously.

"Well, it's officially Christmas now, so we want you to have this." Sutter held out a box covered in dark velvet. Together, he and Josh raised the lid.

Inside was an engagement ring, its setting comprised of three openwork hearts. In the middle, where the points of the three hearts met, a small diamond nestled.

"We want you to marry one of us," Josh said. "Make this official."

Kendall smiled at them both, her eyes bright with happy tears. "Marry *one* of you?"

"Legally, that's all we can do. We were thinking maybe later we could have a private ceremony. There's a pastor Brandy knows who might be willing to do a service joining the three of us, here at the house."

"That sounds perfect." Kendall held back her tears as Josh and Sutter lifted out the ring and together slid it onto her finger. "How are we going to decide who it will be?"

Josh and Sutter again exchanged glances. "Well," Sutter said. "We thought maybe it should be me. We thought that maybe my dad would be more accepting if — you know, things appeared less unorthodox."

Kendall nodded thoughtfully. "That's a good idea. I think you're right." She studied Joshua's face carefully. "Are you okay with that? It won't bother you?"

He grinned. "I know in my heart what's true."

Firelight danced in the heart of Kendall's diamond like joy danced in her own. Reclining against the fur, she held out her hands to both of them. "Make love to me," she whispered. While Sutter watched, Josh covered her body with his. He took her slowly, tenderly, all three of them savoring each sweet, delicious moment. When Sutter took his place, even he took his time, uncharacteristically patient and gentle as they celebrated their engagement.

* * * * *

Kendall was in the kitchen early the next morning, stuffing the turkey, when she heard a raised voice in the den. She finished what she was doing, tucked the bird into the oven, then washed her hands and wandered into the den. Sutter was staring at the blank TV screen, flushed and angry, with the cordless phone in his lap. "What's the matter?" Kendall asked.

Sutter shook his head. "My dad. I called to tell him the news and invite him over for Christmas dinner. He proceeded to tell me how you're a gold digger and that there's no way he'll give us his blessing."

"That doesn't even make any sense," Kendall exclaimed hotly. "I'm supporting all three of us right now!"

"He says you don't mind doing that because you know there's going to be a big payoff in the future."

"God, that's ridiculous! How old is your dad?"

"Fifty-two."

"He could easily live thirty or forty more years! He thinks someone would do this for a payoff that wouldn't come until they're in their sixties?"

"I don't think he seriously believes that. I think it's just the fact that I really am making decisions without him. He can't think of any other legitimate reason to object, and he won't come right out and admit that he can't stand that he doesn't control me any longer. Plus, I think he kind of blames you for my—what did he call it? Oh, yeah. Rebellion."

Josh came in and flopped down on the couch, looking from one to the other. "What's up?"

Kendall didn't want Christmas day to be marred because of a self-righteous bully. "Nothing," she assured him with a warning glance toward Sutter. "Nothing at all." She held out her hands to them and smiled. "Come on, you guys. I need help in the kitchen."

* * * * *

Their guests started arriving around noon, and Kendall pushed all thought of Sutter's unreasonable father from her mind. Around three o'clock, the food was ready and she left Josh and Sutter in the kitchen carving the turkey to go mingle with their friends in the living room. She was laughing at something Brandy had said when the front door opened and David Campbell walked in. *I thought that was locked*, she said to herself. Brandy raised her eyebrows questioningly. Kendall shrugged and hurried over to head him off.

"Ever heard of a neat little invention called a doorbell?" she asked lightly when she reached him.

David grimaced. "I'm used to having the run of the place. Sorry." The tone of his voice made it clear that the apology was insincere. "Where's Sutter?"

Kendall grabbed his arm and pulled him through the den and out onto the deck. Her red silk dress didn't offer much protection against the biting wind. She turned to face him, rubbing her arms against the chill. "Look. It's Christmas day, and you have no right to come over here and upset him."

"I don't plan to upset him." David offered her a charming smile, but she wasn't buying it. "I came over here to offer the two of you my blessing."

Kendall's gaze narrowed. "What's the catch?"

David feigned surprise. "Kendall. I'm hurt!"

She waited impatiently, tapping her foot against the weathered boards.

"All right." David dropped the pretense and got right to the point. "I've taken the liberty of having our lawyers draw up a pre-nuptial agreement. You sign that—" he eyed her shrewdly, "And I'll give Sutter my blessing."

"You had them write up a pre-nup on Christmas day." Kendall stated flatly. She couldn't believe the lengths to which this man was willing to go to retain some shred of control over his son's life.

"What's it going to be?" he asked, ignoring her statement.

Kendall thought for a moment. "On one condition."

Here it comes, David thought. *Now we'll see what she's REALLY after.* "What would that be?"

"That you make an effort to be just a father to Sutter. Not his career counselor or his moral conscience—just his father. He very much wants a relationship with you, but not if it means you're going to continue trying to run his life. And—" she watched his face carefully. "You quit pressuring him regarding Josh."

Her answer was not what he had expected. He'd been telling himself for weeks that the woman was after something, and when he found out that his son was going to marry her, he had decided she was after Sutter's inheritance. She couldn't possibly love him—he was still in college, for God's sake, just starting out in life. And this thing with Josh—he refused to think about that. A woman her age ought to want someone established, stable. The only other explanation was that she was after the money. He had thought with a pre-nup in play, she might offer to let him buy her off. But she had agreed to the pre-nup readily, and all she honestly seemed to want was for him to accept this strange relationship. The small part of him that wasn't a cynic tried to suggest that maybe she was exactly what she appeared to be—a woman in love with his son. *That would be all right,* he told the voice, *if it weren't for Josh.*

Kendall watched the play of emotions on his face. He seemed surprised, even disappointed. She strongly suspected that he had thought she would offer to go away for some kind of payoff. The silence stretched. Kendall waited, trying to ignore the cold.

The woman in front of him shivered, and David made a quick decision. "All right," he said slowly. "I'll back off. But no negotiation on the pre-nup. You sign it as is."

He expected her to argue, but Kendall just shrugged. "Fine, David." She pushed past him and opened the door into the den. "Sutter's in the kitchen," she called to him over her shoulder, then walked off and started chatting with someone as though he were already forgotten.

After the way he had imagined this confrontation would go, the whole thing was anti-climactic. He felt as though he'd been robbed. And he hated being dismissed as if he were unimportant. He almost reconsidered his decision and left. A chill gust of wind found its way down his collar and he shivered. Stepping inside, he closed the door behind him. The brief activity gave him a moment to reflect. He had what he wanted now, didn't he? Not exactly, since Josh was still in the picture—but Sutter and Kendall would be married, and with that legality in place people wouldn't question too much the fact that Josh still lived with them. And not a penny of Campbell money would go to her if this marriage didn't work out.

He started making his way through the guests. He was still angry about law school, but he could afford to be patient about that. Let Sutter try his little business. When it failed, he would realize he needed a real job and come back around to his father's way of thinking. David nodded to himself. Yes. This could all still eventually work out the way he had planned. He might as well enjoy the fact that someone else was paying the bills for a change. With that pleasant thought in his head, he almost didn't have to fake the smile on his face as he walked into the kitchen to give his son the good news.

* * * * *

"No." Kendall and Josh sat on the bed watching Sutter pace after everyone had gone. "I don't want that hanging over our heads. You don't have to prove anything to me, Kendall. I won't let you sign it."

"Sutter. If doing this one thing will make this whole relationship more acceptable in your father's eyes, why fight it?"

"That's why." He stopped and glared. "He'll be getting his way again!"

Kendall shook her head. "Not about anything that *really* matters." She looked to Josh for help.

"Think about it, Sutter," Josh offered. "The only way this paper means anything is if there's a divorce." He looked deep into Sutter's eyes. "You know that isn't going to happen. The only way any of us is leaving this relationship is when we die. So he's fooling himself. When he passes away, his money goes to you, which means Kendall will have access to it despite him. And if anything happens to you, it will go to her. So in the end, this is just a paperwork exercise that strokes his ego. I say, if stroking his ego gets him off our backs, then stroke away."

Sutter sat on the bed. "I don't understand this whole 'gold digger' paranoia anyway. Dad's well-off, but like you said, he'd have to die for any of it to come to me. He certainly doesn't have the kind of wealth someone would be willing to wait thirty or forty years for."

"Exactly." Kendall stroked his arm. "It's just a power play. The only thing is, he doesn't realize it really gives *us* the power. Because we won't have to worry about him anymore."

Sutter frowned. "I guess you're right. But I still don't like it."

Kendall reached behind her and began pulling down her zipper. Josh took over, finishing the movement and pushing her dress off her shoulders. "What *do* you like?" she murmured seductively. Following her lead, Josh unfastened her strapless bra and dropped it to the floor, baring her chest. "This?" Kendall lifted one breast and bent her head, teasing the tip of her nipple with her tongue.

Sutter groaned. "That's not fair."

Kendall grinned wickedly. "All's fair in love and war." She closed her mouth on her nipple and sucked noisily, Josh grinning at Sutter from behind her.

Sutter groaned again and leaned forward, taking the other nipple in his own hot mouth, still watching her. Kendall leaned back, raising her hips as Josh slipped her dress off over them. She reached down and began unbuttoning Sutter's pants.

Josh pulled them off him as Kendall pressed him back against the bed. "Okay, okay, I like!" he admitted.

"This?" Kendall asked, joining Josh at his crotch, their tongues tasting his cock.

"Damn," Sutter murmured. "Definitely."

Kendall parted his buttocks and slipped a finger into his anus. "And this?" she whispered huskily. She had discovered that this turned him on almost as much as it did her.

"All of it," Sutter moaned. "Whatever you do. Whatever you want me to do. I like it all."

"Good," Josh whispered, and Sutter gasped as he brought his hand up and inched one of his fingers in alongside Kendall's.

They pressed their lips tightly to either side of his cock, moving rapidly up and down in unison. Kendall enveloped his tingling head in her mouth on one upstroke, Josh the next, as their fingers probed and found that special place inside his ass that made him cry out, "God, yes! Yes!"

He thrust a finger into Kendall's pussy and wrapped his hand around Josh's cock, pumping both furiously as he climbed to fulfillment. He lost himself in the sensations — his, Kendall's, Josh's. It still amazed him, how wonderful it felt to him and to Josh, to touch each other, to make each other come. He felt their bodies quickening as his mind melded with theirs, releasing his own sensations and thoughts into the flow. Kendall's legs tightened around his hand, her cunt spasming. Sutter's cock erupted as Josh's warm essence flowed down to coat his other hand. He was vaguely aware of Kendall screaming out his name, of two hungry mouths lapping up his seed, then he was drowning in a red tide of ecstasy as their triple orgasms blended into one mind-blowing ride.

Chapter Twelve
Key to the Kingdom

Kendall and Sutter were married in January by a Justice of the Peace in a small service with Josh and Brandy as witnesses. On Valentine's Day, the three held a private ceremony in their home, where Brandy's progressive pastor joined Josh, Kendall and Sutter in what they considered to be their true marriage. Sutter had designed their wedding rings—perfect in their simplicity. Eighteen carat gold engraved with three interlocking hearts, their names etched on the inside of each band. A large group of friends attended, celebrating the union with them long into the night. The next Monday, Kendall filed the paperwork to have her last name legally changed to Reed-Campbell.

The men graduated in May—Josh was class Valedictorian. He accepted a great job with the biggest architectural firm in town, his designs hot properties even before he started, his portfolio having already been shopped out by his employers. For the next two months, Kendall and Sutter worked their butts off. Kendall had purchased the rest of the building in which her shop was located, and within a month they had put in a workshop and storefront for Sutter. July he spent creating, building up a small inventory. Life seemed to be settling down for them at last. David Campbell had kept his word—his relationship with Sutter was friendly and undemanding.

He even stopped by occasionally to have dinner with the three of them.

As Kendall drove home the first Friday in August, she was feeling pretty good about the way things were going. Sutter had announced that morning that he would be opening shop the next week. She pulled into the driveway and hopped out of the car. She wiped her brow and hurried up to the front door. God, it was sweltering. She couldn't wait to get into something light and cool. She opened the door and stepped over the threshold. In a heartbeat, Sutter and Josh were at her side — closing the door behind her, startling Kendall by reaching out to take off all her clothes.

"What's this all about?"

"I thought we'd celebrate the grand opening," Sutter explained, wiggling his eyebrows suggestively. Then Josh led her into the kitchen and they ate, her body filling with desire as she sat there naked before them. Their devouring glances and erotic thoughts had the seat of her chair damp with her juices by the time they had finished the meal. She sat quietly while they cleared the table. When they were done, her husbands stripped and Sutter lay down on the kitchen table. Kendall raised her eyebrows. This was something new.

"Come here," he demanded. Kendall approached and Josh helped her up onto the table, turning her so that she was crouched over Sutter, her lips above his towering cock. Sutter's fingers slipped into her pussy. Kendall moaned and began licking his shaft eagerly. After a few moments, he guided her hips down to his face, tasting her cunt. She gasped as he buried his tongue inside her and began rubbing her clit, his fingers wet with her juices.

Josh's hands massaged her buttocks, warm and slippery. When he teased her anus, she moaned again. Sutter's hands, cold after Josh's, parted her cheeks as Josh slipped his forefinger inside her. "Mmmm." Kendall took Sutter's balls in her mouth, nipping a little, the way he liked. He squirmed on the table and wiggled his tongue inside her. "Oh, yes," Kendall murmured.

Josh twisted his finger in her anus, pulling gently at the edges. In the past few months, Kendall had discovered that this was one of her 'hot spots', and the carnal lust only this type of play engendered in her rose abruptly, filling her belly. She sucked Sutter's balls. Hard. "Yeah, baby," he murmured into her pussy, squeezing her ass. "I like that!"

Josh removed his finger and tested the opening with his thumb. As he had hoped, it slipped in with a minimum of resistance. "Oh, yes," Kendall moaned, as he began stroking in and out. "Yes, Josh." She took Sutter's cock in her mouth.

Oh, God! She still couldn't get over the excitement that electrified her body when the three of them joined. Her mouth on Sutter's cock; Josh's thumb in her ass and Sutter's tongue in her pussy. She writhed as her pleasure mounted. As usual, she had to hold back to keep from climaxing before they did. They could make her come so easily. It wasn't fair!

Josh lubricated his other thumb and eased it into Kendall's anus. Sutter groaned as Kendall abruptly loosed his cock and raised her head. "Oh," Kendall mumured, as Josh pulled his thumbs apart — spreading, stretching. "Josh!" The light dawned, and Kendall's voice cracked as she asked, "Are you going to — "

"Yes."

Kendall released a low sob of anticipation. Finally. She'd been waiting for this a long time. Sutter had fucked her ass several times now, but she had never had Josh that way. He kept insisting she wasn't ready yet. And he was probably right. Josh had the thickest cock she had ever seen. But that was one of the reasons she wanted it so much. She wanted to feel that massive shaft in both the dark places that gave her so much pleasure.

Josh worked her gently several more times, then released her. He carried over the bench from the table in the breakfast nook and knelt on it, covering himself copiously with the lubricant. Sutter held Kendall's cheeks wide as Josh pressed the tip of his shaft against her.

Kendall was excited, spasming as she anticipated his thrust. The contractions and relaxations of her anus were like little kisses being administered to the tip of his cock. Josh groaned, wanting to plunge into her immediately. Instead, he eased himself in, watching as his head disappeared inside her.

Kendall whimpered and Sutter moaned as Josh shared the image with them. *Give it to me, Josh,* Kendall demanded through the bond. *ALL of it.*

"God, Kendall!" Caution abandoned, he grasped Kendall's hips and drove himself forward.

Kendall took Sutter's cock head deep inside her throat, stifling her whimpers as Josh's cock stretched her to the point of pain. Abruptly, warm lubrication streamed into her crack, and as Josh pulled out and pushed back in slowly, it became easier. The pain morphed into an insistent, buzzing need. Kendall pumped her mouth up and down on Sutter's cock, fondling his balls with one hand. On impulse, she reached between his legs with the other and found his anus, penetrating it quickly with one finger, then moving that finger in and out as she imitated Josh's rhythm in her ass.

"Fuck!" Sutter yelled, pure pleasure streaking through the bond.

Kendall increased her pace on Sutter's cock and Josh followed suit. "Oh, yeah, Kendall," Josh moaned as she squeezed her anus on his cock and her pussy on Sutter's tongue. "Yeah, baby." Kendall moaned, loving how the friction made his stiff rod hot inside her; made her ass throb delightfully. *But he still hadn't given her EVERYTHING.*

Kendall rocked her hips back forcefully, burying Josh deep inside her. He couldn't believe she had taken it *all*. "Kendall, yes," he gasped as she rocked forward and then drove her hips back again. "Yes!"

One, two, three more times she moved, and then the world froze as Sutter jetted into her mouth and Josh's cock pulsed between her cheeks, filling her ass with his warmth. Sutter reached up and wrapped his arms around her waist, pressing his mouth tight against her, tonguing her pussy as she climaxed.

Afterward, they lay on the rug in the living room, contemplating the fire. Josh turned to her abruptly. "I want to try something." Kendall raised her eyebrows. She felt him mentally dive into the bond, pushing through the flow, sending more of his presence into her than ever before. "What—Oh!" A pulse of pleasure contracted her pussy. "How did you—oh, God!" Her pussy pulsed again, and she arched her back. "Josh!"

Without warning, her nipples began to tingle. She started to reach for them, but Josh grabbed her hands and held them. Sharp bursts of fiery sensation throbbed at their tips and she moaned. "Oh, Josh." Abruptly, her anus tingled, then her pussy, then her nipples again. Then all three, and Kendall arched and writhed as a fierce climax ripped through her.

"Show me," Sutter demanded. Josh grabbed his hand and drew him through the link, showing him how to fuck their wife without even touching her.

"Oh, God! Josh, Sutter, please."

Sutter's eyes glittered. "Please what, Kendall? Stop?" he teased. She shook her head frantically, arching again as another powerful orgasm made her entire body shudder. Sutter and Josh shared a wicked look as they made themselves comfortable.

"All night long," Josh promised Kendall, licking his lips as she writhed on the floor, her orgasm washing over them. "All night long." As their joined minds filled her consciousness and erotic sensations blossomed without warning throughout her body, Kendall felt herself falling into oblivion for the second time in her life as orgasm after orgasm rocked her long into the night.

Kendall woke up the next morning physically exhausted. She'd never realized until Josh and Sutter how much of the body orgasms utilized—seemingly every muscle, as they now ached, and much of her energy. But as she lay there and watched her husbands sleep, a slow smile spread across her face.

Kendall immersed herself in the bond and began exploring, sending little tendrils of thought-sensation out. Even in sleep, their bodies responded and Kendall was able to learn what she needed. When Kendall felt she was ready, she began working on them in earnest. Shortly, their eyes flew open and they gasped in unison as semen spewed from their cocks, Kendall watching with a satisfied smile. When it had passed, they wrapped their arms around her and covered her in kisses. "That wasn't fair," Josh murmured.

Unfortunately, it wasn't physiologically possible for Kendall to repeat the process only seconds later the way they could with her. However, they were vigorous and in their prime, and there were certain things that could make them hard again in a relatively short amount of time. Reaching out, she found their cocks and feathered her fingers over them lightly. When they moaned, she urged them to face one other, their bodies nearly touching, and rubbed their cocks against each other. Sutter especially found this very erotic. Within minutes, he was hard again, and Kendall was sending electric pulses of pleasure through his cock, his anus, his nipples—as they had done to her. He groaned as another orgasm shivered through his body. Josh's shaft burgeoned as he watched, and moments later Kendall had him arching against the floor as well. Kendall sat back. "Take a rest, boys. But not too long." She grinned wickedly. "I'm not done with you yet."

They spent the rest of that day naked. Every time they became aroused, Kendall used her new-found abilities to make them come as they had her, until late that evening they fell into a deep sleep on the living .room rug, limp and exhausted.

On Sunday, Kendall woke ravenous. They had eaten nothing since Friday night but sandwiches around noon the day before. She put together a big breakfast, enjoying the experience of cooking in the nude. The guys wandered in eventually, and Kendall sat between them, toying with their cocks while they ate their fill. By the time they were done, she had them rock-hard. Kendall took their hands and pulled them back into the living room, back to the rug. She had driven them crazy the day before, making them come over and over again without touching them. But she had also driven *herself* mad, denying herself their touch. She craved physical contact.

Josh's eyes were dark with passion as she lay back on the floor and spread her legs for him. He eased into her slowly, relishing the feel of her warm, wet flesh on his cock. Kendall sighed with contentment.

"Sutter." Josh sent a thought, and the other man grinned. Sutter grabbed the lubricant. Positioning himself between their legs, he found Josh's anus with his finger, then sprinkled his cock with the oil and guided it in. "Oh, yeah," Josh murmured.

Kendall wrapped her arms around Josh's neck and her legs around them both, bringing Sutter in tight against Josh. Sutter moaned and began stroking in and out, pushing himself deeper and deeper into the narrow canal. His breathing quickened in time with Josh and Kendall's. Kendall closed her eyes. She reached under her hips with her hands. Sutter's pace increased — deep, powerful thrusts that drove Josh into her. Using her elbows as additional support, she pushed her hips up, meeting each plunge with a thrust of her own. "Oh, God!" Sutter's world narrowed to the place where their hips met. Heat rising, hips melding, becoming one — he roared as their triple orgasms flooded the bond.

When he came to himself again, his first sight was Kendall staring to the right of his shoulder with a horrified expression on her face. Turning his head, Sutter saw his father. Fists clenched. Red-faced and trembling.

"How the hell did you get in?" Sutter asked.

Josh raised his head at the remark and started involuntarily at the sight of Sutter's father standing over them.

Kendall stared at Sutter in amazement. When she had opened her eyes and seen David Campbell standing there, her first thought had been that Sutter would be a stammering fool when he realized. He felt the thought and favored her with an irritated glance.

David's reply was harsh through tight lips. "I have a key, remember?"

Sutter backed out of Josh and rose, standing casually. "Actually, no. I had forgotten." He held out his hand. "Do you mind?"

David opened and closed his mouth several times, shaking with fury. Finally, he dropped the key into Sutter's hand.

"Thanks."

Josh and Kendall shared delighted glances. They couldn't believe how confident Sutter was — unintimidated, finally, by his father.

Sutter raised his eyebrows. "Did you need something?"

David stared at his son in disbelief. "Is that all you have to say?"

Sutter's voice remained light. "Dad. This is our home. You invaded our privacy. I'm sorry if what you saw shocked you, but I don't owe you any apologies."

David's lips were pressed together so tightly they were white. Josh rolled off of Kendall and the two of them lay there watching. David's glance drifted their way, dripping daggers at them. "That's it," he said. He looked back at Sutter, speaking through clenched teeth. "We're through. I don't ever want to hear from you again."

Kendall started to protest, but closed her mouth at a calm, silencing thought from Sutter.

"If that's the way you want it."

David couldn't believe what he was hearing. This — he searched for a word. Defiant. This defiant man wasn't his son. Even in the past few months, his son had stood up to him only passively, through Kendall. He glanced at the floor again, at the woman who was watching Sutter with pride. Curse the day she had ever entered their lives. He could have brought Sutter around eventually, if it hadn't been for her. His gaze narrowed. *Well.* His fury was fading, replaced with cold calculation. *Seems like a change of plans is in order.*

Without another word, he swept past Sutter and out the door.

Josh stood up and wrapped Sutter in a bear hug. "I can't believe you did that, man."

Sutter trapped his face between his hands and kissed him lingeringly. "I love you, Josh. I'm not ashamed of that any more." He turned to Kendall, holding out his hand to help her up and pull her into their embrace. "Kendall was right. We have to be true to ourselves. Since I started doing that, I've never been happier."

Kendall's eyes filled with tears. "I'm so proud of you, but — what about your dad?"

Sutter shrugged. "He'll get over it. He's been fighting this relationship for years. He's got to realize eventually that he can't change anything. Once he comes to terms with it, he'll be back."

Kendall nodded, but as Sutter embraced them both again, she and Josh shared a concerned glance. She, for one, wasn't convinced.

Chapter Thirteen
Revisiting the Past

It was three months later, the first week in November, and Kendall was singing along with the radio, getting ready to open the shop. Every time she thought she was as happy as she could possibly be, something happened that made life even better. The day before, Sutter had made his first huge sale. There had been an anxious time before he built up an inventory and garnered a reputation, when Josh and Kendall had to talk him out of giving up nearly every day. But he had finally made a small profit in September and a significantly larger one in October. Then on Thursday, two clients had gone into a bidding war over a fresco he had done of the Three Fates. The final bid had been for seventy-five hundred dollars. The future looked promising.

Kendall sighed and frowned. The only thing marring that future was David Campbell. He and Sutter were no longer talking. He had spoken to Sutter once after their confrontation to let him know that he had written him out of his will. Kendall had suspected that might happen, but she wished things could have been different. Especially with the holidays approaching. As confident and self-reliant as Sutter had become, she knew that he loved his father, and for his sake she would have liked for the man to be a part of their lives despite his flaws. But there was nothing Kendall could do, so she pushed the thought away and began humming cheerfully again.

Mid-morning, she was in the midst of placing an order when she felt a sharp pang of anxiety. *What the HECK?* She went on with her conversation, making sure the vendor she was speaking with had her order for framing parts correct. After she hung up, she sat nibbling at her lip. She sent out her mind, testing her links with Sutter and Josh. They both seemed all right.

She began working on the necklace she had been piecing together, twisting thin silver wire into a filigree cage for a garnet she wanted to attach. She continued to feel uneasy, and tested the bond a second time. Sutter was fine, but Josh seemed agitated, though she couldn't get a feel for what was wrong. She sensed he was hiding something from her. *What was it?*

As the day wore on, her anxiety grew. When Brandy showed up a few minutes late for work, Kendall jumped on her verbally until Brandy's wide eyes and open mouth registered and Kendall stopped abruptly. "Brandy. I'm so sorry. I can't believe I just did that."

Brandy shrugged it off. "I knew you didn't mean it. What's wrong?"

"I don't know." Kendall fidgeted nervously with the pencil she was holding. "I've just had this strange feeling all day long. I think something's wrong with Josh, but I can't tell what it is. He's cluttering the bond so Sutter and I can't see." She and Sutter had eaten lunch together, his worry seeping into her through the bond, disturbed to know that neither one of them could break through.

"Do you want to leave?"

Kendall glanced at her watch. It was only three-fifteen. "Wouldn't do any good. He's still at work. I can't go up there, how would that look? I'm sure it's nothing too serious. Probably just something he'd rather wait and tell us about this evening." She turned and headed back to the register. "I think I'm just over-reacting because he's making us wait."

Brandy nodded thoughtfully. "Well, if you want to go ahead and leave at five, that's fine with me."

Kendall smiled at her friend. "Thanks, Brandy."

* * * * *

She knew something was wrong even before she pulled into the driveway. Sutter's car was there—he had stopped by around four o'clock to let her know he was closing shop early and heading home. But Josh's car was missing, and during the drive out Kendall had felt Sutter close his thoughts to her abruptly. The bond hummed with tension. She jumped out of the car quickly and nearly ran to the front door. When she opened it, she found Sutter sitting in the living room in the dark. She flipped on the light. "What's wrong?"

Sutter looked up, his face red with anger. "Josh is in jail."

Kendall stared at him blankly. "What?"

"In jail," he repeated. "I called my father, but he wouldn't even speak to me." He looked ragged. "We have to find a lawyer, Kendall. Get him out of there."

Kendall walked over and collapsed onto the sofa. "What for? What happened?"

Sutter shook his head and jumped up, pacing the floor like an angry tiger. "Embezzlement. They say he's stolen money from the company accounts and the accounts of several of the partners." He met Kendall's gaze, his pupils dilated with worry. "Electronically." He finally let go of his barrier and his thoughts came rushing in — memories of the prank they had played on his father.

"Oh, no." Kendall dropped her head back against the cushion, then sat up. "Wait. They can't use that against him. Josh was a juvenile then. Juvenile records are closed, aren't they?"

"Supposedly." Sutter continued pacing. "What are we going to do?"

Kendall's gaze narrowed. "First we find a lawyer. Then there's someone I want to talk to."

* * * * *

Kendall waited impatiently in the anteroom of David Campbell's office. She had been surprised when his secretary had said he'd be glad to see her, but he was making her wait, and her fury was mounting. Finding a lawyer on a Friday night had been a difficult task, and though they had finally acquired one, Josh was still in jail. Apparently, they would hold him until the bail hearing. And unfortunately, the lawyer had informed them that Josh's juvenile conviction could be used against him after all. It seemed that juvenile records were not automatically sealed, as she'd always thought. After an individual turned eighteen, they had to go to court and specifically request that the record be closed. Then, depending on the nature of the crime (or crimes) and the judge, they could still refuse to seal the records. Of course, Josh had never even thought about it.

The door to David's office finally opened. "Sorry that took so long, Kendall," David said, his tone falsely apologetic. "Business." He ushered her in and closed the door behind her. Kendall took a seat in one of the richly appointed leather chairs in front of his desk as he sat down and looked at her with feigned sympathy. He rested his elbows on the blotter and brought his hands together. "Now. What can I do for you?"

"I know you did this," Kendall said quietly.

David leaned forward, resting his chin on his steepled hands. "I'm afraid I have no idea what you're talking about, Kendall."

Kendall met his gaze calmly. "Josh didn't steal that money," she said. "But you know who did." She leaned back into the chair, trying to appear at ease. "I think you hired someone to do this. To frame Josh and get him out of Sutter's life."

David nodded thoughtfully. "I don't doubt that you want to believe that. However—" He spread his hands and shrugged. "I had nothing to do with this." He shook his head. "I won't deny that the prospect of Josh being out of the picture suits me just fine." He watched Kendall shrewdly. "Perhaps now, you and Sutter will quit playing at this alternative lifestyle and settle down. Raise a family." He stood and came around, leaning against the front of his desk, arms crossed before him. "He can go back to school. I doubt that I can get him into Harvard again, but there are other—"

"That's not going to happen." Kendall was glad that her voice did not betray her strain—the words unhurried, delivered casually—though she was seething inside. "Sutter isn't a lawyer, and he doesn't want to be one. He's a very good artist. An artist with a wife *and* a husband, however much you dislike that. And we'll both be waiting for Josh when he comes home, if you somehow manage to get away with this." She smiled, a surprisingly difficult thing to do when her stomach was churning. She was putting on the performance of her life. "But I'm not going to let that happen."

David raised his eyebrows. "Really."

Kendall nodded.

His gaze narrowed. "He's done this before, you know. He did it to me."

Kendall smiled again. This time it was easier. "So. You *do* know the details."

David shrugged nonchalantly. "I'm a lawyer, Kendall. We talk."

"He was just a boy then, David. And he and Sutter were angry."

David pushed himself away from the desk and leaned over Kendall, resting his hands on the arms of her chair. His face was only inches from hers. "He's *still* a boy, Kendall." He moved until their lips were nearly touching. "They both are." His gaze traveled over her hair, her face, her body. "You need a *man*." He waited, expecting to have thrown her off balance.

"Like you, David?" Kendall murmured seductively, allowing her lips to graze his as she spoke.

Astonished, but not necessarily displeased, David shivered. *What an interesting new development!* "Yes," he whispered.

Kendall burst out laughing. David stepped back, face flushed. Kendall shook her head as her laughter trailed away. "What bothers you more, David?" She stood and put her purse over her shoulder. "The image of Sutter and Josh having sex, or the fact that Sutter is happy in a way you've never experienced?"

Something flashed in the depths of his eyes. Kendall caught the briefest flicker of some deep emotion. Then it was gone. "I think it's time for you to go, Kendall." He spoke in a bland, measured tone, but his hands were clenched at his sides, their knuckles white. God, the woman infuriated him! He had tried to throw her off-balance, and she had somehow turned it all around. He began to understand why Sutter loved her. She was a force of nature. For the first time in his life, he felt a sense of loss. He could have had something like this, years ago—he pushed away the thought.

"Yes, it is," Kendall was saying. She tilted her head and looked him in the eye. "It's been a pleasure, David. Really." And she meant it. She had cracked David Campbell's façade, and there was something lurking underneath. Something she might be able to use. She smiled, and this time it was completely genuine. "But I'll be back." She brushed imaginary dust from his shoulder with one hand. "Trust me on that." She turned and sauntered from the room.

In her car, she pondered David's reaction to her question. What *had* she seen in his eyes? Not anger. Not fear. Not jealousy. Not any of the things she would have expected. Kendall chewed at her bottom lip. *What was it?* Then it came to her. Guilt. *Why guilt?* She knew instinctively that he had no qualms whatsoever about setting up Josh. And she was now more convinced than ever that he was behind it.

Shaking her head, she started the car and backed out, heading toward the shop. She needed to talk to Brandy. Brainstorm. David Campbell felt guilty about something, and Kendall was determined to figure out what.

Chapter Fourteen
Best Laid Plans

Kendall sat in her old apartment, sipping the hot chocolate Brandy had given to her. She had related to her best friend everything that had taken place in David's office. Brandy was now staring thoughtfully into the fire.

"Refresh my memory," she said. "Josh and Sutter pulled the hacking prank when?"

"The summer they were fifteen," Kendall answered.

"Because Sutter's dad had banned the friendship."

"That's right."

"But he gave in pretty easily after Sutter swore they weren't physically involved."

Kendall nodded.

"So it was kind of like token resistance."

Kendall thought for a moment. "Well, yeah. I guess so."

"But then when they got to college and were still so close, he started freaking out. Putting on more and more pressure to break them up. Especially at the beginning of their senior year."

Kendall nodded again. She couldn't quite see where Brandy was going with this. "But after I became involved, and Sutter and I got married, he seemed okay with things. He was mad about Sutter not going to law school, but he seemed to have resigned himself to that."

"Until he walked in on the three of you that weekend."

Kendall studied her friend. "What are you thinking?"

"I don't know. There's something niggling at the back of my mind. Let's talk it out." She tilted her head thoughtfully. "At first glance, he just seems homophobic. But the pattern, his reactions—they're kind of odd. I'm sure he suspected it might get physical back when they were in high school." She stood and began pacing, thinking aloud. "But he backed off. Then he got agitated again when they started college, and was freaking by the time they were seniors. Then he backed off again when you came along and married Sutter, even though it was obvious Sutter still had a relationship with Josh." She stopped and frowned. "I know walking in on the three of you would be quite a shock, but in the end, why would he care? I mean, he knew the three of you were living together—probably even knew about the second wedding."

"You think so?" Kendall interrupted.

Brandy looked at her pityingly. "Trust me. David Campbell *knew*."

Kendall nodded, her mind racing. "So then—assume that he had convinced himself nothing of that sort was going on between Sutter and Josh. That it was only me they had sexual relations with. Sutter and I made it even easier for him to delude himself when we got married for the sake of public appearance."

"Exactly." Brandy began pacing again, her brow furrowed in concentration. "Then he saw something that took away that self-delusion." She stopped again. "But he didn't react quite the way I would have expected. Didn't call them names or act disgusted, right?"

Again, Kendall nodded. "Just angry."

"Right. And not so much about the actual act, but more like he was just furious with Sutter for not complying with his wishes. As a matter of fact, if Josh were to end up in jail, he would welcome Sutter back into the fold. Reinstate the will. Be all involved in his life again, right? Wouldn't even mention what went on with Josh."

Kendall nodded slowly. "Yes, I think he would. But that's because he will have finally gotten his way."

"No." Brandy shook her head. "It's more than that. If there's one thing I know, it's people."

Kendall forced a smile. "I know, that's why I needed your help figuring this thing out."

"A true homophobe—especially a controlling, old-school guy like David—would be disgusted. Repulsed. He'd *never* welcome a son back with open arms after seeing him like that, even with the guy gone and a heterosexual marriage in place. He wouldn't have any respect for Sutter. Or you, for that matter—a woman who would condone that, even participate."

"What are you saying?"

"For him to feel guilt, if that's what it was—" She settled on the couch next to Kendall, a serious expression on her face. "I think he's done it. Experimented. Probably in college. Or maybe it was involuntary, who knows?" She tossed her hair over her shoulder. "Anyway, he thinks it's his fault." She grabbed Kendall's hands and squeezed them tight. "That's where the guilt comes from. He thinks he's responsible for Sutter and Josh's relationship. That's why he can forgive and forget if Josh disappears."

Kendall was stunned. "This is — wild speculation!"

Brandy bared her teeth — the grin of a bloodhound on the scent. "So let's find out if I'm right."

* * * * *

Brandy pulled into the driveway of a neat little cottage painted a buttery yellow. Despite the fact that it was November, colorful plants brightened the landscape — flowering kale, variegated ivies. Normally Kendall would have admired the view, but her stomach was in knots. She held back as Brandy marched up the sidewalk. "I'm not sure we should be doing this."

Brandy turned and planted her hands on her hips. "Kendall. David Campbell is a criminal defense attorney. A good one. If he did this, the case against Josh is going to be airtight. Figuring out his motivation is the only thing that's going to give you any leverage."

Kendall continued reluctantly up the walk. Brandy rang the doorbell. A moment later the door opened.

"Brandy!" The petite, plump brunette who answered hugged Kendall's friend tightly. "I'm so glad you called."

"Me too, Joy." Brandy smiled and gestured toward Kendall. "This is my friend, Kendall Reed-Campbell."

Joy smiled and held out her hand. "Nice to meet you."

Kendall shook her hand and the woman ushered them into the house.

When she had them ensconced in the screened porch off the kitchen, a pitcher of iced tea at the ready, she asked, "So. What is this research project you needed help with?"

Brandy blushed. "I may have misled you a bit." Joy Daniels had been Brandy's instructor her freshman year, a mentor who eventually became a friend. They had kept in touch until Brandy had graduated in May, but hadn't talked for the past few months. "I wanted to ask you some questions, actually. About David Campbell."

Joy's eyes widened. "What about David?"

Kendall sat and listened uncomfortably while Brandy related as briefly as possible the details of Kendall's relationship with Sutter for the past year. Brandy had told her Joy would have to know the whole story, but it was still unnerving to hear it related to a perfect stranger. "Anyway," Brandy said when she had finished, "I knew you and David had dated his senior year—my mom mentioned it. I was wondering if you knew anything."

Joy looked at Kendall, her expression veiled. "What exactly are you planning to do?"

"I don't want to hurt him," Kendall insisted. "But I know he's behind this. Maybe if I understand what's going on and confront him, we can clear this up. In the absence of that..." She thought long and hard before she said the next few words. She could tell that the woman still cared a great deal for David. Finally, she decided she owed it to her to be completely honest. "If what we think is true, and there's any way to use it to *make* him confess, then that's what I'll do."

Joy stared down at the tablecloth. So many years ago. And David was still trying to control the people in his life. She had seen him recently, at a charity banquet. He hadn't noticed her, but she had watched him and known that he was as miserable as ever—trying so hard to be the person his dad was. Denying himself. She couldn't stand the thought of helping this woman to hurt him, but what would happen to Sutter if David won? Another Campbell generation passing down bitterness and anger. Maybe it was time to shake up David Campbell's world. "I could see him doing this. He was always a control freak. In college, they nicknamed him 'Ruthless'. He had to win at everything, no matter what the cost. I had hoped he would mellow with age. Obviously he hasn't." She sighed. "I don't know if this is the right thing to do, but—there *was* this guy our senior year. Jason Weir. He was David's roommate. Of course, David didn't live on campus. He had a beach house. Didn't need a roommate, financially speaking, but he's the kind of man who always wants someone around. An audience. Sometimes I would get this strange vibe from the two of them." She shrugged. "I don't know the truth. If there *was* anything between them, it was very discreet."

Brandy leaned forward eagerly. "Do you know where he is?"

Joy nodded, somewhat reluctantly. "He teaches at a college in the Fort Worth area. Astronomy. I—I think I have his address." She stood to get it. "You know, I never thought anything of it, the fact that he used to write to me occasionally. We were never that close back then, but after he moved I would get the odd letter, and he always asked about David. Haven't heard from him in a couple of years, though."

She returned with an envelope in her hands. "Here's the envelope from the last letter he sent. The address isn't necessarily current, but it should help." She handed it to Kendall. "Just—don't do anything rash, okay? I—" She shook her head. "I shouldn't care, but I do."

Kendall took her hand. "Joy. He's my husband's father. Sutter loves him. I don't want to see him destroyed. I just want him to let us live our lives. If I do find out something that could be damaging, I'll use it for leverage.

But if he calls my bluff—" She hesitated, then admitted, "I won't go public. I couldn't do that."

Joy's expression brightened. "Thank you for that."

"Just wish me luck. Josh and Sutter and I—we belong together." Beside her, Brandy nodded emphatically.

"I don't have any hang-ups about things needing to be traditional. Some of the strongest relationships I've ever seen have been out of the ordinary." Joy smiled. "And Brandy's the best judge of character I know. So, good luck and—will you let me know how it turns out?"

Brandy hugged her tight. "Definitely. We won't lose touch this time, either. I promise."

* * * * *

Kendall's plane landed at Dallas-Fort Worth International Airport forty-five minutes ahead of schedule. She settled into a seat to wait for her ride. By calling DFW information, she and Brandy had been able to use the address Joy gave them to obtain Jason Weir's phone number. Kendall had talked to him briefly on the phone, once again using a cover story to get in the door. She said she was doing a write-up on David Campbell for Galveston's *Big G* magazine—a Man-of-the-Year piece— and wanted to interview friends from his past. Jason had expressed surprise that David had even mentioned him and questioned the need for her to actually come to Fort Worth, suggesting they conduct the interview over the phone. Thinking fast, Kendall had told him that the magazine was going to pay to fly in a couple of the interviewees for the big night, and preferred a face-to-face interview, with photos, in order to make their decision. Jason had gone quiet, but had finally agreed.

"Kendall Reed?" She glanced up to find a tall, slender gentleman with a great smile and twinkling eyes standing at her side.

"Yes." She picked up her bag and stood. "Jason?"

He held out his hand. "Nice to meet you." He took her bag and started for the exit. "How was your flight?"

"Not bad." She glanced at her watch. She had only been waiting for about ten minutes. "You're early."

Jason smiled. "I only live fifteen minutes from the airport. I called to check on the arrival time, and found out you guys were ahead of schedule." He held the door open for her and led the way to his car.

They made small talk during the short drive. The weather, the recent meteor shower, what it was like living so close to a noisy airport. Not too bad, it turned out, since the house was not in the direction of the usual flight paths. When they arrived, he carried her bag into the house and led the way into the kitchen. "Coffee, tea, soda?" he asked.

"Coffee would be great."

"Good. I started a pot before I left." Jason poured their drinks and brought them to the table. "So. What do you want to know?"

Kendall looked down at the table. "I haven't been honest with you." She looked up. He had such an open face and friendly demeanor. "I feel terrible about lying to you, but I'm desperate."

Jason frowned, his dark brows nearly meeting in the middle. "What's this all about?"

For the third time in four days, Kendall related the story of her life for the last year. When she was finished, Jason looked sad. "He still doesn't get it." He shook his head. "I wondered about your story. I didn't think David would ever mention me to any journalist." He sipped at his coffee. "Yeah, we were involved."

Kendall's heart did a flip. She never dreamed it would be this easy. He noticed her expression and laughed. "Thought you'd have to drag it out of me, huh?"

Kendall nodded.

"I've never been ashamed of what I am," Jason said. "David was the one. His dad had very particular ideas about what he wanted his son to be, and Dave bought into all of it. When he realized we were attracted to each other, he fought it tooth and nail at first. But David—he very seldom denies himself anything. He finally couldn't stand the suspense anymore. He invited me over to his place one night to experiment, and a few days later I was his roommate."

"How did it end?"

"We graduated. David went away to Harvard. I moved here and pursued my Master, then my Doctorate. I never had any delusions that it would be a permanent situation. The only reason our relationship lasted as long as it did was because we lived a double life. Nobody ever suspected." He grinned ruefully. "That was important to David. We never would have been able to keep it up, long-term. I guess Joy saw through it, though."

"I think Joy is the kind of person that sees things other people miss," Kendall said. "Plus, you wrote to her after you left, asking about David. She said she never thought about it until we asked, but I think in the back of her mind, she may have suspected."

"I suppose so." He frowned. "David really did care for her, I think. He broke up with Joy when I moved in. He could have hung onto her. He dated other girls while we were together, to keep up appearances. But I think he regretted losing her."

"He must have been a very different person then," Kendall mused.

Jason looked surprised. "Why do you say that?"

"Because you and Joy so obviously still care for him. This may sound callous, but I can't imagine anyone feeling so strongly about the man I've come to know in the past year."

"David had a very generous nature. He just buried it under all the crap his dad used to feed him." He sighed. "I don't know. Maybe he *has* changed. Living a lie all these years — it has to affect him.

"For a while there, I thought he might be all right. Joy wrote to me — it must be thirteen, fourteen years or so ago — that he was doing a lot of charity work. Donated money for an entire wing to a hospital. Sponsored some kid at that Whitecliff school his son went to."

Kendall's breath caught. "What did you say?"

"He used to do charity —"

"No." She leaned into the table. "He sponsored somebody at Whitecliff?"

Jason nodded, taken aback. "Yeah. So what?"

"Do you know the kid's name?"

"I can check. I still have Joy's letters." He left the room and came back carrying a small wooden box with a hinged lid. He rifled through the envelopes, opened a couple and read the first few lines. "Yeah. Here it is. Reed. Joshua Reed."

Kendall sat back, dumbfounded. Suddenly everything clicked into place. "I can't believe it."

"Believe what?" Jason's eyebrows rose. "Wait a minute—your other husband, you said his name is Josh? *That* Josh?"

Kendall nodded.

"Damn. I'm surprised Joy didn't say anything."

"I'm not sure we ever mentioned Josh's last name specifically, or that he had gone to Whitecliff. Brandy just told her the stuff that had gone on in the past year." Kendall picked up her coffee, warming her hands. The temperatures in Galveston had not been that cold lately, but Fort Worth had been invaded by a cold front the night before. "So. David Campbell has a homosexual relationship in college, and he's ashamed of it. Then—"

"Not exactly ashamed," Jason interrupted. "It just wasn't *done*. And he knew his father wouldn't approve."

"Okay," Kendall mused. "So he doesn't really think it's wrong, but he knows society doesn't approve. And he's very concerned about what society thinks. Then he sponsors Josh at Whitecliff, Josh and Sutter become really close, and he starts thinking Sutter's following in his footsteps. And that bothers him because by this time, he's trapped in his own father's role, and he isn't capable of letting Sutter be any different."

Jason nodded. "So he cuts them off in high school, but Sutter swears it's not physical, which he *wants* to believe, so he backs off."

"But when they get to college, he becomes more and more anxious, because that's when he became physically involved with *you*. He thinks history's repeating itself."

"Then *you* come along, and marry Sutter, and he thinks everything's going to be okay. You guys are presenting an appearance he can live with—"

"But he walks in on us, and he can't pretend he doesn't know any more." Kendall sipped her coffee. "And he feels responsible. For Sutter's inclinations, and for the fact that he's the one that brought Josh into Sutter's life. So he decided to try to get rid of him once and for all." Kendall shook her head in disbelief. "God. It's like a bad soap opera."

Jason laughed. "We're right, though. I know we are."

"How does this help us, though?"

Jason looked at her for a long time, then stood again. He came back and pushed a large manilla envelope into her hands. "Open it."

Kendall opened the envelope and flipped silently through the pictures inside. She looked up at Jason. "He let you take pictures?"

Jason chuckled. "*Let* me? Hell, it was his idea. I told you, once he tried it, he enjoyed it. David Campbell really throws himself into things. We even made a home movie. You can't have that, though." He grinned wickedly.

"You're so—comfortable with yourself," Kendall observed. "I'm probably more comfortable with my situation than either Josh or Sutter, but I could never hand these pictures to a complete stranger and sit there so nonchalantly while they looked through them."

"You're not such a stranger." His good humor faded, replaced by the wistful sadness she had sensed earlier. "I love David, you love his son. We didn't get our chance at happiness, but I'll do what I can to make sure you get yours."

Kendall put the pictures back in the envelope and fastened the brad. "What if he calls my bluff?"

"You couldn't go public, could you?"

Kendall shook her head. "Like I told Joy, I don't want to destroy him. Just wake him up."

"Good luck with that," Jason said. "David never listened to anyone but his father." He watched her with sad eyes. "I don't know, Kendall. The best advice I can give you is—don't let him see that you're bluffing. If he believes you'll expose him, your Josh may just have a chance."

Chapter Fifteen
Bringing up Baby

The hardest part was telling Sutter. She had to let him know what was going on and how she wanted to handle it. At first he didn't believe her — wouldn't even consider the possibility that David was behind Josh's arrest. He kept insisting that the police had just made a mistake. That they would look at the evidence and realize that they had arrested the wrong man.

Kendall felt like she was living a nightmare. She woke up every morning feeling like she was going to throw up. Brandy thought it was the flu, Kendall was convinced it was the stress. Days became weeks. Kendall finally went to the doctor the day before Josh's hearing. She had a bad feeling about the hearing, and wanted to get something to settle her stomach. Later that day, she met Brandy for lunch.

"Sutter still hasn't come around, huh?" Brandy asked, watching as Kendall played restlessly with the soup she had ordered.

"No."

Brandy was worried about her friend. She looked pale, tired — wrung out. And she'd hardly eaten anything in the past few days. "Look, just show him the pictures. He's got to believe you then."

Kendall shook her head. "I just—I don't want to go that far unless I absolutely have to." She made a face and pushed her soup away. "I'll be back in a second."

Brandy grabbed her wrist as she stood. "What did the doctor say? Is it flu?"

A brief flicker of some unidentifiable emotion passed across Kendall's face. "No, but he did give me something for it."

Brandy watch with concern as her friend made her way to the bathroom, a nauseated expression on her face. "So what are you going to do?" Brandy asked when she returned.

Kendall rubbed at her temples. "Josh's bail hearing is tomorrow. If we can get him out on bail, then I'll tell him what's going on, and maybe between the two of us we can convince Sutter."

"What if bail's too high? Or they deny it?"

Kendall's eyes were bleak as she met Brandy's concerned gaze. "Then I guess I'll have to show him the photos, whether I want to or not." Brandy reached out and covered Kendall's hand with her own. They sat that way for a long time, Brandy offering silent support and Kendall lost in her own thoughts.

Her premonition regarding the bail hearing turned out to be valid. The prosecutor claimed Josh was a flight risk. Supposedly, ticket purchases had been made by Josh on-line, and the tickets had not been found. The prosecutor argued that there was no way to be sure they had frozen all the accounts Josh had access too, and that there was a good chance he had stashed tickets and money so that he could run if he got caught. Unfortunately, the judge agreed. Sutter and Kendall returned home that evening devastated. Josh had been denied bail.

Kendall woke at two in the morning to find the other side of the bed empty. She crept down the stairs and found Sutter sitting in the living room, staring at cold embers. She sat down beside him and held out the envelope. "I know how hard it is to believe everything I've been telling you, Sutter." She wanted to cry, but couldn't. "That's why I've been waiting. Hoping that you would—" She shook her head, unable to continue for a moment, choking back tears. Finally, she went on, "I didn't want to show you these, but maybe they'll convince you."

She watched him—scared to death, her heart in her throat. If he reacted the wrong way, this could break them. He opened the envelope and thumbed through the pictures, his face blank. Kendall could feel nothing through the bond. He was shielding. When he had finished, he looked up, his eyes fierce. "He *did* do this, didn't he?" He threw the pictures to the floor. "Damn him!"

Kendall reached out to touch his arm, but he backed away. "I'll kill him," he said, his voice colder than ice.

"Stop it!" Kendall's tears finally fell. "He made mistakes, but they can be fixed. He thought he was doing the right thing."

Sutter grabbed her by the shoulders. "How can you defend him? Josh is in *jail*! Do you know what it's been like for him?"

Kendall's voice shook. "I feel everything he feels, Sutter."

He blinked. He stared at his hands as though just realizing what he was doing, and let go abruptly. Kendall rubbed at the red marks on her arm. "I'm sorry." His voice shook.

Kendall swallowed the lump in her throat. "I know this is hard, Sutter. He tried to destroy us. But you have to forgive him. He's your father."

Sutter shook his head.

"We have to confront him, Sutter. But you need to be able to tell him you understand. That you forgive him."

"I can't do it. Besides, he'll never admit he framed Josh. How can he? It would ruin him just as surely as these pictures would."

Kendall wiped away her tears and wrapped her arms around his neck. "I think there's a way around that." She ran her fingers through Sutter's hair. "Do you trust me, Sutter?"

He closed his eyes and buried his face in her hair. "You know I do."

"Then let me go to him. He can fix this, I know he can. But it has to be different after this. We have to make him a part of our lives."

"He doesn't want that, Kendall."

"I think he does." She tilted his head up so she could see his eyes. "Please. Trust me."

"What about Josh?"

"If this works, he'll understand. He'll work through it—we all will."

Sutter finally nodded. Kendall took his hand and led him back up the stairs to bed.

* * * * *

David let Kendall into the office and waved her to a chair. They sat staring at one another for several minutes. She didn't look good. Her eyes were dark. She looked tired, unhealthy. He felt an uncharacteristic pang of concern. After all, the woman *was* his daughter-in-law.

Finally, Kendall reached into her bag. She pulled out a manila envelope and slid it across the desk. "What is this?"

"Just open it." Devoid of any feeling, her voice was a raspy whisper.

David opened the envelope and looked at the top photo. All color drained from his face. Without looking any further, he set the stack on his desk and met her gaze with empty eyes. "I suppose these aren't the originals."

"You suppose correctly."

"How did you find out about this? Where did you get these?" He studied her face while he waited impatiently. Kendall's determination certainly hadn't diminished, but she definitely seemed exhausted. Another unaccustomed emotion darted through him. Regret? David looked away. It wasn't his fault. Sutter and Josh should have done as he said long ago. All this was a result of *their* refusal to listen.

"Let's just say I'm a very determined woman who happened to know the right people to ask," Kendall answered.

David rubbed his face with his hands. "I knew I should have burned those pictures."

Kendall sighed. "I wish you could see that there's nothing wrong with what the three of us have." She watched him for a moment. "There's nothing wrong with you, either. Or with the relationship you and Jason had."

David raised his head and stared. "Things were different then."

"Exactly." Kendall leaned forward earnestly. "Things *have* changed. Yes, there are people now who don't approve of the three of us. But there are quite a few who do. They understand that we don't choose who to love. Love chooses us. True love isn't a conscious act—it's something that just happens." David stood and began walking back and forth. "If we don't care what people think, why should you?"

"Because it—it *is* wrong."

"Do you honestly believe that?" Pausing, she watched him pace. "I don't think you do. You're just afraid of what people will think, and how Sutter's reputation might affect yours." She sighed heavily. "Look, I don't want to destroy you, David. I didn't even want to *hurt* you, but you left me without a choice. I can't let you do this to Josh. You're not just hurting him, you're destroying me and Sutter as well. Your son and his wife. Is that what you really want?" Kendall stood and walked over to the window, watching seagulls wheel above the gulf. "I know how hard it must have been." She turned and met his eye. "It's one thing to feel like there's something wrong with you. Like you've passed that something on to your son. It must be even harder when you know you're responsible for bringing Josh into Sutter's life."

David stopped in his tracks. "What are you talking about?"

"I know you sponsored Josh at Whitecliff."

Appearing genuinely shocked for the second time, David made his way around the desk and sat in his chair heavily. "Who—who told you? Those records are confidential. Sutter even told me Josh tried to hack into them and couldn't."

"Jason knew. Through Joy. They've been keeping in touch with each other all these years." Kendall had gone to visit Joy right after she returned, telling her what she had found out and promising again that it would only be a bluff. It had turned out that the reason Joy knew about David's sponsorship was because she had been the second-grade teacher who recognized Josh's potential and had asked David for help. She had then gone on to pursue an advanced degree, winding up eventually as Brandy's professor at the college. It really was a small world.

"Joy." David shook his head. "Can't trust *anybody*, damn it."

"She cares about you, David." Kendall leaned back against the windowsill and crossed her arms. "She likes for people to know that there's more to you than meets the eye."

David had regained his composure, his features a familiar mask of calculated disdain. "It was a tax write-off."

Kendall shook her head in wonder. "You really do think that the slightest sign of compassion will be taken for weakness, don't you?"

David suddenly felt tired. More exhausted than he'd ever been in his life. He couldn't seem to remember a time when he hadn't been fighting—with his father, with Sutter, with himself.

Kendall saw his carefully cultivated public mask slip again. She caught her lip in her teeth. Making a sudden decision, she moved over to the desk and knelt beside him.

"I want you in our lives, David. Sutter loves you. Josh and I could at least *like* you, given a chance."

David turned to face her, disbelieving. "Why?"

"Because we love Sutter, and he loves you, despite everything. He's your son. And—I shouldn't tell you this. I haven't even told Josh and Sutter yet—I wanted to wait until Josh came home." She hesitated. She was deeply bitter over what David had done, but she felt as though she were very close to breaking through that brittle façade. She took a deep breath. "I'm pregnant, David, and I'd like our child to know his or her grandfather."

David hadn't felt anything so remarkable in years. *I'm going to be a grandfather!* He felt like laughing, but to his surprise, tears came to his eyes. *What have I done?* he thought. The stress Kendall was going through. Now, while she was pregnant— "You can't possibly want me involved. Not—" he swallowed, then forced himself to admit, "Not after what I've done."

Kendall nearly broke down at the admission. "We forgive you, David."

He shook his head. "I can't—I can't accept that. What about the boys?" David asked. "At the very least, I can't imagine *Josh* would ever be able to forgive me for this. Or—do they know?"

"They're not boys anymore, David. They're men. And yes, they know. Everything."

David's face reddened and he glanced at the pictures. "Everything?"

"All of it," Kendall said softly. "And they don't care."

"That can't be true."

"They're angry, yes. But David, without your sponsorship, Josh would never be where he is today. You felt guilty for bringing him into Sutter's life, but you actually made two of the best things that ever happened for him possible—Sutter and his education. And I keep telling you—Sutter loves you. You don't stop loving someone just because you're angry with them. The anger fades—love doesn't. The nature of our relationship means that his love for you is a part of us, as well. We're willing to forgive everything, David. Clean slate. If you stop this now."

David leaned back in his chair. "How? You can't expect me to go to the police and say I did it. It would ruin me."

Kendall stood and moved back to the chair in front of the desk. "You paid someone to do this, I assume."

David nodded.

"Where's the money?"

David eyed her suspiciously, but finally answered. "Dummy account. Just like the stunt Josh pulled."

"Have him transfer the money back, then come forward and expose it as a prank. Make it worth his while. Do you have enough influence to get him off with probation?"

David's gaze narrowed. "Probably. But he'd have to have a legitimate reason for pulling the prank in the first place."

Kendall had thought of that. "Does he have a job?"

David's eyes gleamed. "I don't think so. Lives in a dump. Hacks for grocery money. He diverts a million dollars, and charges me a couple hundred." Kendall raised her eyebrows. "Doesn't have a degree. Like Josh when it comes to computers, self-taught. Hard to find a job in the field nowadays without a degree."

"Would he be interested in a legitimate job? Say, designing firewalls or writing security programs?"

David was nodding. "I'm getting it. He could say he did it for the recognition. To get job offers. And he waited a while to come forward because he wanted it to be high-profile."

"Will it work?"

"It's going to sound like a pretty stupid stunt, but people pull stupid stunts all the time. You wouldn't believe the strange things I've heard in court over the years. We can make it fly. I have an associate who would be happy to represent him for me. Especially if the guy's cooperative. And he will be." David smiled. "I can get him hired. One of my clients owes me a favor. For a little financial incentive up front, probation, and a job offer — yeah, I think the guy will do it." David stared admiringly at his daughter-in-law. "You really are remarkable. I can understand what Sutter and Josh see in you."

Kendall's smile was bright with relief. "I just want to live my life with the two people I love."

Epilogue
New Year's Eve

Kendall tapped a spoon against her glass. "Could I have everyone's attention, please?"

Faces turned her way from around the large table. All their old friends were present, along with David and a couple of new ones—Joy and Jason. Kendall smiled as Josh and Sutter came to either side and put their arms around her. "We have an announcement to make." She beamed as she looked around. "You all know I'm pregnant, but we found out today—it's twins!"

"Omigosh!"

"Congratulations!"

"Cheers!"

Happy chatter broke out all around. Several people came up to hug Kendall and congratulate all three of them. When the crowd had thinned, David stepped up. Everything had gone according to plan. His hacker had come forward. With every penny of the diverted funds returned, the associate David had mentioned had been able to arrange a plea bargain with the District Attorney's office on behalf of his client, and the man would begin working for Datatech Industries in February. David's relationship with Sutter and Josh remained tense, the three of them still finding their way aro

und several issues, but Kendall made him feel at ease. "That's wonderful news," he said.

Kendall gave him a hug. "I'm glad you came." He appeared more relaxed than she'd ever seen him. More *real*.

David shrugged. "It's hard," he admitted. "Facing people you've hurt. But I love my son and I don't want to lose him. He and Josh and I—we're working things out."

"I know." She smiled, and glanced down the table. "Have you spoken to Joy? Or Jason?"

David frowned. "I—don't feel comfortable."

Kendall cupped his cheek with her hand. "Dad—" David still found himself surprised at the sense of contentment he felt when she called him that. "Don't waste any more time. You've wasted far too much already."

David's jaw dropped. Kendall was probably the only person that could tell him something like that and get away with it. He shut his mouth.

She smiled. "There's unfinished business between the three of you." She patted his cheek. "Finish it," she commanded.

David shook his head. "You are—"

"Right," Kendall insisted. David glanced down the table. Joy was in animated conversation with Jason, her face bright and beaming. She wasn't the slender young imp he had dated in college, but she still looked beautiful to him. And Jason—he swallowed. He couldn't think about that right now. He turned back, to find Kendall watching him shrewdly. "I'll try, Kendall, but—not tonight."

She looked as though she were going to protest, but finally nodded. Raising her glass of sparkling grape juice, she said, "Happy New Year, Grandpa!"

David raised his own glass to hers. *Maybe it will be,* he thought. *This year, just maybe it will.*

The End

Enjoy this excerpt from
SYMPHONY IN RAPTURE
© Copyright Rachel Bo 2004

Chapter One: Overture
(Introductory music for an opera, ballet or oratorio)

Michelle paused in her evening walk, admiring the old McMurtry home. The new owners had done quite a bit in the few weeks they'd been there to restore its stately beauty. Simply having the grounds cleared, weeded and trimmed had revived vestiges of the residence's former elegance—the beauty of a profusion of yellow climbing roses was now visible, and huge blush-colored hibiscus blooms glowed in the early sunset.

Michelle smiled and continued on. Grander and larger than the other homes in this small historic district, the lady McMurtry certainly deserved to shine. Happily, the new owners appeared to agree. As she rounded the corner and began walking along the building's north side—the side nearest the street—the clear notes of a piano drifted from an open window. Michelle quickened her pace and stopped just outside the window, peering between the bars of the wrought iron fence into a room beyond the sash.

A man sat at the piano, playing a composition Michelle did not recognize. The music tugged at her heart, an intricate medley—both sad and joyful, bright and somber. Michelle closed her eyes and let the sounds engulf her, feeling a bittersweet nostalgia wash through her.

Nicholas looked up from his playing to see a woman standing on the sidewalk outside his window—hands wrapped around the fence's wrought-iron bars, head tilted slightly, eyes closed. The sight moved him deeply. Why, he wasn't sure. When he was conducting, or playing an especially emotional piece of music, he often glimpsed people in the audience, similarly engrossed. But this was different. Nick felt an immediate connection to her. She wasn't simply enjoying a pleasant-sounding string of notes. The music had touched her soul. Nick had become particularly adept at reading people, and could see this in the woman's face — in the slight upturn to her lips and the narrow furrow between her lush eyebrows. As the setting sun burnished her dark curls with golden highlights, Nick found himself tempted to go out and invite her in, stirred by yearnings he hadn't experienced in a long time; an immediate chemical attraction. That in itself was unusual for him. But there was more. He was curious about her and that surprised him, for it had been ages since anything or anyone had piqued his curiosity.

Abruptly the music stopped. Michelle opened her eyes, only to find herself staring into the sharp, blue scrutiny of the player. Heat rising in her cheeks, Michelle let go of the fence and stepped back, trying to look away but unable to tear her eyes from his intense gaze.

"Don't go," the man said. He smiled. "Come around to the door. I haven't had a chance to meet any of the neighbors yet."

Michelle considered. Across the street, Mr. Jennings mowed his yard, the missus supervising from her swing on the verandah. A few houses down, Jason Matthews laughed, his dog chasing him while he pushed his skateboard along the sidewalk. There were plenty of people out and about. Granted, the guy was a stranger, but there could be no harm in standing in his front yard in broad daylight, introducing themselves. She nodded. He turned away, and she retraced her steps to where the wrought-iron gate stood open in front of the house, then crunched her way up the gravel drive to the front door.

The stranger was waiting for her on the porch, dark tan contrasting handsomely with his flaxen hair, beige slacks, and white shirt. He held out a hand. "I'm Nicholas Duquaine, but my friends call me Nick."

Michelle's heart skipped a beat. "Nick Duquaine?" she echoed. "The conductor? You composed *Hearts of Atlantis Bleeding*, right? It's one of my favorite symphonies."

Nick smiled, but seemed uncomfortable with the recognition. "Yes, and thank you." He glanced pointedly at his outstretched hand.

"Oh, sorry. I'm Michelle. Michelle Wright. Welcome to the neighborhood!" Embarrassed, Michelle felt heat rising in her cheeks again as she reached out, but even more disconcerting was the flood of warmth that invaded her loins.

Their hands met, and a wall of desire blew through Nick like a storm front. He maintained the electrifying contact as she tried to draw away.

"Are you a musician?" he asked.

"Yes, I am. How did you know?" An erotic tingle raced along her arm and danced over her ribs at the continuing touch, settling in her crotch as a buzzing need.

Nick smiled. "Just a feeling." He shifted slightly as his penis stirred restlessly.

Acutely aware of Nick's warm palm against hers, Michelle said. "I play the guitar, mostly. I'm a singer in a local band. You probably haven't been here long enough to hear of us, but it's called *Something Wild*. We're actually fairly successful, on the club scene—" She realized she was babbling and took a deep breath.

Surprised at his intense attraction, but enjoying it immensely, Nick suddenly realized that the woman was also highly aroused. The pulse in her neck jumped rapidly. Her silk blouse tented slightly in the area of her erect nipples. Nick's thighs tightened as a smoldering fire kindled below his belt. "Come in for a minute."

Nick's grip on her hand was gentle but insistent. Flustered, Michelle tore her gaze from his and looked out toward the street. "I really should be getting—"

"I promise not to bite." Nick reached out with his other hand and captured her free hand in his, forcing her to meet his gaze once again. He flashed a dazzling smile.

The need invading Michelle's body shocked her. She had not dated in several years. As a matter of fact, she had given up on relationships entirely, especially since Angela's death. It had not been a difficult choice. She hadn't been even remotely attracted to anyone in a long time. But Nick's advances were rapidly awakening an appetite Michelle wasn't sure she wanted to reacquire. *For God's sake,* she told herself, *He can't possibly know. He isn't asking you out on a date. He's just a new neighbor, being friendly.* Still, she felt as though she was diving into an ocean without a life jacket as she bit her lip, then nodded slightly. Nick backed through the doorway, pulling her in after him, then nudged it shut with his foot and led her down a long hallway to the left. Through an open door, Michelle glimpsed a piano, and a moment later they were standing in the music room.

A Steinway dominated the corner of the room nearest the open window. A divan graced the opposite wall and a couple of overstuffed chairs and a side table were arranged near a marble-faced fireplace. A mahogany cabinet filled the space near the door. Shelves covered the last wall, and on those shelves were a variety of gleaming musical instruments and well-worn cases. It was a room any musician would love.

"What do you think?" Michelle turned to find Nick watching her with an intense expression.

"It's beautiful," she answered. Her stomach fluttered like a schoolgirl's. *You're being ridiculous,* she thought. To hide how awkward she felt in his presence, she walked over and pretended to study the assortment of flutes, penny whistles, and recorders on one shelf, her footsteps echoing loudly on the stone floor. "Do you play all of these instruments?"

"At one time or another," Nick replied. He sat at the piano. "Would you like me to finish that piece?"

"Oh, yes!" Michelle sat on the edge of one of the chairs as Nick began playing the composition that had captured her attention on the street. Michelle closed her eyes and floated away with the music.

Nick studied her as he played. She was probably about thirty-five. Her long, dark lashes grazed cheeks pinkened by a natural blush — she wore very little makeup. Nick liked that. He allowed his gaze to travel over Michelle's body, admiring her smooth skin, the generous cleavage, the little pooch to her belly just visible beneath the sleek line of a silky black skirt. Her shapely legs were bare, and she wore dress flats rather than heels. A prickling sensation invaded Nick's groin, a rushing pulse stiffening his cock as he watched her. He pictured himself rubbing its firmness over the curve of that belly, pressing its rigid length into the soft flesh, with nothing between them.

When the last note had faded, Michelle reluctantly opened her eyes. Nick was staring at her with a hungry expression that both aroused and frightened her. *Get a grip*, Michelle thought. *He's just another guy.* An unexpected trickle of moisture seeped from her crotch, dampening her panties, and her nipples began to tingle. "I-Is that something new?" she stammered.

The wolfish look on Nick's face disappeared, replaced with careful indifference. "Yes." He sat quietly on the piano bench, watching her for a moment, then stood abruptly. "I have a guitar. Would you like to play for me?" he asked.

"I couldn't," Michelle demurred.

"Why not?"

Michelle shrugged. "I'm not in your league. I write pop-rock, mostly upbeat stuff. It's nothing special. I'd be embarrassed to play for you."

Nick frowned. "That's too bad. If your music ever embarrasses you, then perhaps you're not playing the right music." He approached the chair she was sitting in, halting a couple of paces away.

"Well," Michelle didn't know how to respond to that. She stood. "I guess I had better be going."

"Not yet."

Startled, Michelle stared at her host. "What?"

Nick could feel mutual attraction dancing between them like electrified air just before a lightning storm. "Come here," he whispered hoarsely, somehow knowing that she would.

Dangerous, a voice in her head whispered. *Not a good idea*, it insisted. Nevertheless, Michelle found herself taking the two small steps necessary to stand before him.

Nick reached out and ran his fingers through the tawny curls on either side of her face, then stroked the curve of her shoulders. He drew his hands along the bare skin of her upper arms. Goosebumps raised on her flesh as his thumbs grazed her breasts—near, but not touching, the straining nipples whose dark tips were just visible beneath the thin fabric of her shirt and bra. Michelle shivered, searching Nick's eyes. No longer bright, sky-colored pools, they now resembled the deep, grey-blue of storm-tossed waters. Nick held her gaze.

A part of her was urging Michelle to stop this now, to leave. Another part was silently willing him to touch her taut peaks—and they tingled as she felt his thumbs against their tips, kneading gently. She held her breath as Nick brought his lips close to hers, hovering—the possibility of their touch a searing key that slipped beneath her defenses, unlocking the portal to a tidal wave of long-denied passion. Unable to believe what she was doing, yet driven by an overwhelming longing, Michelle closed her eyes and parted lips that hadn't been kissed in five years. Nick's flesh met hers, his agile tongue invading, probing; his plunging strokes stirring up deep reservoirs of physical need.

Nick felt slight tremors shuddering through Michelle's body. He deepened his kiss, wrapping her in his arms. Tentatively at first, then more insistently, Michelle met his tongue's advances with her own. Each darting exploration set tendrils of pure pleasure tugging at Nick's groin like the strings on a marionette—his cock pulsing, expanding. He reached down and slid Michelle's silky skirt up. She moaned and made as if to pull away. Nick lifted his mouth and whispered huskily, "Please, let me touch."

Michelle couldn't open her eyes—*wouldn't* open her eyes and meet the gaze of this perfect stranger whose every wish she suddenly wanted to grant. She felt him waiting, and then his hand feathered along her thigh, until his fingers found the damp cotton between her legs. She shuddered, but leaned into him, burying her face in his chest. Firm, rotating pressure on her clit through the damp fabric escalated her need. Michelle moaned, parting her legs slightly.

Nick wanted so badly to bury his bulging cock inside her pussy, but knew instinctively that although she was responding amazingly to his touch, that would be going too far. He eased the crotch of her panties aside.

Michelle gasped as two of his fingers slid between her warm, wet lips, flexing inside her. The feel of another person's strong, firm fingers inside her throbbing sex after so long drove her wild with desire. They slipped in and out, his rough thumb circling her clit. "Oh, God," she gasped, digging her fingers into his shoulders.

"Come for me," he urged.

Feeling like a strumpet, but too desperately aroused to deny herself, Michelle reached out with her left leg, seeking the chair she'd been sitting in. Her toes brushed against it, and she cocked her leg, resting her foot in the seat—offering unimpeded access to her crotch. "Yes," Nick whispered. "That's it." Nick dipped his fingers in and out. "Come for me, baby." Moaning, Michelle drove her hips forward, taking his fingers deeper. Nick responded by burying them inside her and holding them there, wiggling his fingertips.

Michelle gasped. His long, slender fingers played her pussy like the keys of a piano—his fingertips against her G-spot stimulating her to the brink of orgasm, then pulling her back—again and again. Her own warm juices trickled down her right thigh, a tickling progress that heightened the exquisite pleasure. She couldn't remember ever being this wet, this horny. She tried to subdue a desperate sob, but failed. She felt Nick bury his face in her hair, chuckling softly. This time, when she felt herself teetering on the peak of fulfillment, she was rewarded. Twisting his hand as he plunged his fingers repeatedly into her, he pressed his free hand against her tailbone. The extra support immobilized her hips, and she found herself moaning over and over as he bored into her, deeper and deeper, his knuckles massaging the slick tissue surrounding her vaginal opening, while his fingers danced in her pussy. Finally, she came; bucking frantically as penetrating spears of pure delight lanced through her body until her knees gave way.

Nick moved the hand at Michelle's back, wrapping it around her waist to support her. The dripping, succulent pussy milking his fingers sent waves of pleasure through his crotch; in the next instant, a pulse-pounding release soaked his pants, despite the fact that he'd been trying to hold back.

Nick supported Michelle until she regained her feet. When she was steady, she felt his fingers withdrawing slowly from her cunt, and she stifled a moan, feeling abandoned. Nick continued to hold her as she tried to gather the shreds of her non-existent composure. "I only promised not to *bite*," he whispered playfully in her ear. Michelle kept her face buried in his chest. She couldn't believe that she had reacted so wantonly with a total stranger. "Hey," Nick took her chin in one hand, tilted her face up to his. "It's okay," he insisted. "It was something we both wanted."

Michelle took a shuddering breath. "I have to go," she murmured, voice husky. She pushed away, straightening her skirt with shaking hands.

Nick grabbed her arm. "Come to dinner with me tomorrow night."

Unable to bring herself to meet his gaze, Michelle stared at the marble floor. "I don't think that's a good idea." She swallowed, hoping to clear her thoughts and strengthen her voice. "This was a mistake."

"Why? I enjoyed that." He cocked his head and leaned toward her, trying to get her to meet his eyes. "I think *you* enjoyed it."

"You're a total stranger." Michelle shook her head. "I know everybody says this, but I'm not usually like that—"

"I know." Nick kept his voice calm, reassuring. "Neither am I. But there's something between us…" He reached out and ran a finger along her cheek. Startled, Michelle steeled herself and was relieved that she was able to keep from trembling. She reluctantly raised her eyes to his. "I won't be a stranger, if you let me take you out to dinner tomorrow." His tone was tender, cajoling. "I'd like to get to know you."

Michelle wanted to say no — *needed* to say no — in order to maintain any semblance of personal dignity. She couldn't do it. Her so recently pleasured crotch was already hungry for more. She glanced down, and was gratified to see the dark stain on Nick's pants. Apparently, he *had* enjoyed the encounter as much as she. And when she returned his gaze, the eyes staring into hers were open, honest, unembarrassed. There was no hint of condescension or judgment.

"Are you sure?" she asked. "You're not just asking me to make me feel better about this?"

Nick laughed. "No, I'm asking you to make *me* feel better." His expression became serious. "Because I know if I don't, I'll wonder for the rest of my life what this might have led to."

Michelle swallowed. Either Nick was sincere, or he was a major player who knew all the right things to say, and she didn't want to get involved. But that didn't jive with what she'd read in the newspapers. According to them, *music* was his mistress. Not that she particularly trusted the media. In the end, she let her reawakened needs overrule good sense and said, "All right."

Nick offered his hand, and she took it, allowing him to lead her from the room to the front door. Michelle stepped over the threshold, but Nick pulled her back for a quick kiss. "Until tomorrow," he whispered against her lips.

Michelle nodded, not trusting herself to speak. She turned and hurried down the steps, working hard to keep from stumbling on weak legs as she walked down the driveway, acutely aware of Nick's eyes on her. Nick brought his hand, still damp with her juices, up to his nose, inhaling deeply as he watched her walk away. The heady scent was intoxicating, and even before she passed out of sight, he was planning the next night's seduction.

When Michelle had reached the street, turning past the fence line and shielded from Nick's gaze by vegetation, she could hardly keep from running home, feeling sure that every neighbor she passed knew exactly what she had been doing.

About the author:

Rachel Bo began writing at a very early age. Previously published in local newspapers (general interest articles) and science fiction/fantasy magazines (fantasy fiction), Rachel was unable to devote the time necessary to completion and marketing of novel-length Double Jeopardys. After years of working in the science field of the private sector, creativity won out and Rachel switched to a part-time job in order to devote herself to writing. Within six months, she had made her first book sale. Though her projects to date have technically been contemporary romances, most do incorporate elements of fantasy, science fiction, or the paranormal. Rachel is also working on several full-blown fantasy stories and a menage-a-trois series.

Rachel welcomes mail from readers. You can write to her c/o Ellora's Cave Publishing at 1337 Commerce Drive, Suite 13, Stow OH 44224.

Why an electronic book?

We live in the Information Age—an exciting time in the history of human civilization in which technology rules supreme and continues to progress in leaps and bounds every minute of every hour of every day. For a multitude of reasons, more and more avid literary fans are opting to purchase e-books instead of paperbacks. The question to those not yet initiated to the world of electronic reading is simply: *why?*

1. *Price.* An electronic title at Ellora's Cave Publishing runs anywhere from 40-75% less than the cover price of the <u>exact same title</u> in paperback format. Why? Cold mathematics. It is less expensive to publish an e-book than it is to publish a paperback, so the savings are passed along to the consumer.

2. *Space.* Running out of room to house your paperback books? That is one worry you will never have with electronic novels. For a low one-time cost, you can purchase a handheld computer designed specifically for e-reading purposes. Many e-readers are larger than the average handheld, giving you plenty of screen room. Better yet, hundreds of titles can be stored within your new library—a single microchip. (Please note that Ellora's Cave does not endorse any specific brands. You can check our website at www.ellorascave.com for customer

recommendations we make available to new consumers.)

3. *Mobility*. Because your new library now consists of only a microchip, your entire cache of books can be taken with you wherever you go.

4. *Personal preferences are accounted for*. Are the words you are currently reading too small? Too large? Too...**ANNOYING**? Paperback books cannot be modified according to personal preferences, but e-books can.

5. *Innovation*. The way you read a book is not the only advancement the Information Age has gifted the literary community with. There is also the factor of what you can read. Ellora's Cave Publishing will be introducing a new line of interactive titles that are available in e-book format only.

6. *Instant gratification.* Is it the middle of the night and all the bookstores are closed? Are you tired of waiting days — sometimes weeks — for online and offline bookstores to ship the novels you bought? Ellora's Cave Publishing sells instantaneous downloads 24 hours a day, 7 days a week, 365 days a year. Our e-book delivery system is 100% automated, meaning your order is filled as soon as you pay for it.

Those are a few of the top reasons why electronic novels are displacing paperbacks for many an avid reader. As always, Ellora's Cave Publishing welcomes your questions and comments. We invite you to email us at service@ellorascave.com or write to us directly at: 1337 Commerce Drive, Suite 13, Stow OH 44224.

Discover for yourself why readers can't get enough of the multiple award-winning publisher Ellora's Cave. Whether you prefer e-books or paperbacks, be sure to visit EC on the web at www.ellorascave.com for an erotic reading experience that will leave you breathless.

Printed in the United States
29857LVS00008B/148-204

9 781843 609513